KEVIN
and the Dream Stealer

M.D. GRIFFITHS
With Todd Warden-Owen

Illustrations by David Wilson

This edition published by Mega-U July 2006
First Published by Mega-U 2006
Copyright © Mega-U 2006

MD Griffiths has asserted his right under the Copyright, Designs and Patents Act 1988 to be identified as the author of this work.

All correspondence to:
Mega-U
The Megacentre, Bernard Rd, Sheffield, S2 5BQ
www.mega-u.com

ISBN: 978-0-9551322-0-9
0-9551322-0-7

Illustrations by David Wilson
Cover and internal design by Creator Art / www.creatorart.com

You are Special!

Thank you to:

Chris Denham - for your creativeness and friendship.

Dave Gilpin - for your inspiration.

David Wilson - for illustrating so beautifully.

Gill Booth - for your chatter and comments.

Glenda Tue - fer yer right way wi' werds.

Glyn Barrett - for Mr East!

Graham Smith - for your great attitude.

Lisa-Keri - for making life so fun and for putting up with me all the hours spent writing.

Miriam Cox - for reading this first.

Mum and Dad - for encouraging me.

Richard Harris - for your enthusiasm.

Sheron Rice - for saying yes and for your excellence.

Todd Warden-Owen - for your genius and generosity.

And to you all, thank you for giving something precious - your time.

WARNING

BEWARE OF THE DREAM STEALER

Chapter 1

Bullies

The three hooded figures padded silently along the moonlit corridor. The bullies were pleased with their night's work. Not only had they managed to break into the school stores to steal a week's supply of strawberry trifle, but they had also kidnapped the new boy from his bottom bunk.

The new boy's name was Kevin. He was plain looking with orange hair, a freckly nose and a pair of expressive eyebrows that were raised in horror. He was carried like a battering ram, face upwards, through the deserted school corridors. Dangling lamps and modern strip lighting glided silently above him. One bully held his legs, the others his arms. Tall pointy shadows, cast from the bullies hoods, swept across the walls; the shadows made the portraits hanging on them look even more sinister than they already were. He was carried clumsily out into the courtyard, past a headless statue and back in through the teacher's entrance. The sound of approaching voices brought the bullies to a stop. A sharp finger poked him in the side, warning him to be silent.

The voices travelled along the corridor towards them.

'I tell you, they knew how to discipline back then. What a good caning wouldn't cure! A few swishes with a good piece of birch and kids would soon learn to behave!'

'You wouldn't want that *now*, would you?'

'Of course! I'm all for bringing caning back. Ha! That would be an eye opener for some of the little rodents in this school. Not that I need to cane them ... I have other ways ... Don't look so surprised! You'll be amazed what you can get away with here. Last week I

made one of them cut the lawn with nail scissors for six hours. Now that was enjoyable, especially when ... eh ... What is it?'

'I thought I heard something.'

Kevin took a deep breath when the voices came to a stop. This was his chance to escape. He'd recognized the harsh voice of Mr East. He was the cruellest teacher Kevin had ever met, but he'd much rather face the anger of Mr East than what awaited him if he wasn't rescued. And so he screamed. He screamed with every part of his being. He arched his back and kicked his legs, desperate to make a noise through the sweaty football sock that had been jammed into his mouth. Instead, a big fist landed in his stomach with a soft thud, winding him into painful silence.

'What did it sound like? I can't hear a darned thing. Do you think one of the rodents is out of bed at this time of night? They've got more sense than that, haven't they?'

'I tell you, I heard something.'

'Nonsense! It's that hearing aid of yours playing up again, Robert. You should get it fixed. Do it during detentions tomorrow ... I can manage for you. It would be a pleasure to discipline your class, especially ...'

A closing door cut the teachers' voices dead. The bullies let out a snort of relieved giggles and thumped Kevin several more times for good measure. They continued along the deserted corridor, through several sets of double doors, past the science classrooms with their preserved jars of specimens, and finally to an arched doorway. Kevin winced painfully as he was dropped carelessly on the floor and given a kick in the side to remind him to be quiet. Wondering where he was, he looked at the notice pinned to the door, but one of the bullies ripped it off quickly before he could read it. The one who seemed to be the leader lifted the latch, pulled the door open and pushed him onto a flight of stone steps into the darkness beyond. Panic clawed at his stomach. He'd thought the stories had been rumours, horror stories to scare new boys like him. But now it was really happening.

He fumbled at the steps, trying to feel his way in the dark. It wasn't fair. He hadn't even been in his new school for a full day.

More prods and pushes forced him up the spiralling steps, through the doorway at the top and onto the floor beyond. The three hooded figures faced him, breathing heavily. Very slowly and deliberately the smallest held up the crumpled notice that he'd ripped from the door at the foot of the stairs: THE FORBIDDEN TURRET

Chapter 2

Mr East - the one eyed beast

The Forbidden Turret was the first thing Kevin had noticed when he'd arrived at Greystones. It had been raining hard and a social worker, who was more concerned about her last cigarette, had shoved him into a taxi an hour earlier and sent him off to his new school. The taxi driver had caught Kevin looking at the turret in his rear view mirror.

'You don't want to go up there,' he said as he pulled up outside the school gates. 'You don't want to go up there, ever.' He put the taxi in neutral and kept the engine running. 'That's where *they* happened.'

Kevin gazed out of the backseat window. The turret stretched high into the sky and leaned dangerously away from the rest of the school. It looked as if it had been rudely plonked on one corner and was ready to topple over at any moment.

'Where what happened?' asked Kevin, still staring at the turret through the driving rain.

'They'll tell you not to go up there of course,' the driver continued, ignoring him. 'They'll say it's dangerous 'cause it's leaning and all that. They may even tell you it's 'cause the stairs are crumbling or the roof's falling in. Ha! But that's not the *real* reason ... Weather's not very nice for you, is it? First day at your new school as well!'

'Where what happened?' Kevin turned to look at the driver. 'What

happened in the turret?'

The driver twisted in his seat, making the folds in his thick neck bunch up. He licked his lips and opened his eyes wide. 'Murders!'

'Murders?'

'Some say they were 'disappearances', but they were *murders*! Before Greystones was a school it used to be a monastery. One day one of the monks went missing. They never found him. All they knew was that he'd last been seen going up to the turret.

After that the monastery closed down and the building became a library, I think, or was it the mental institution? No, I think it was the library.' The driver scratched his bald head, before nodding. 'Yes, it next happened when it was the library. There was a storm and it was raining ...' As if deliberately, the driver paused. Kevin watched the windscreen wipers moving back and forth. 'It was raining so the librarian decided to work late, hoping the storm would die off, I guess, but it didn't, it got worse. Much worse. So bad, that a huge bolt of lightning struck the tower. That's what made it lean over - not as much as it does now, but that's when it started.'

'What about the librarian?' asked Kevin, intrigued.

'Gone!' said the driver, opening his hands. 'A complete mystery! Everywhere was locked. All they found was her glasses ... on the turret stairs! Coincidence? Maybe. But then there was last year.'

'Last year?'

'The boy - he just vanished as well. The police couldn't understand it. They wanted to shut the whole place down, but the government wouldn't let them. They said there was nowhere else for kids like you!'

'What happened to the boy?' asked Kevin.

The driver laughed and turned back in his seat, 'Listen to me. Telling you all this and probably scaring you half to death. You won't want to go in if I tell you any more. Anyway, it's long gone all that stuff. Long gone. Nothing to worry about!' He pointed to the door. 'If you push that handle up, you can get out. And see those double doors at the end of the path? That's the entrance. If you run fast you shouldn't get too wet.'

'Thanks,' said Kevin, pushing the door open. He grabbed his bag, jumped out and waved goodbye to the taxi. Gingerly, he made his way up the long path, doing his best to avoid the puddles, and onto the front doorstep where he was partly shielded from the rain. He pushed the brass doorbell.

A wicked-looking gargoyle above the door grinned at him. The walls were covered with the ugly stone creatures. Dagger-sharp railings and steel bars on the windows gave the whole place a feeling of being more like a prison than a school.

'Are you the new boy?'

Kevin jumped. He'd been so absorbed in his thoughts that he'd failed to notice one of the front doors open. A boy of roughly his own age, with a very spotty face, was looking at him questioningly. 'If you are,' he whispered, 'then this is your last chance to escape!'

'Hawkins!' snapped a sharp voice from behind the boy. Kevin noticed the boy tense slightly. 'Is it the new boy?'

'Yes!' Hawkins replied over his shoulder.

'Don't "yes" me, Hawkins!'

'Yes, sir! It's him, sir!'

'Well, what are you doing whispering? Let him in, boy.'

Hawkins pulled the door back a little further. It was old and thick and hard to open.

'Don't say I didn't warn you,' he whispered as Kevin pressed past into the dimly lit hallway beyond.

Kevin put his bag down on the black and white tiles which stretched across the floor like a giant chessboard. A gallery, made of dark wood, ran along three sides of the upper walls and a large ornate chandelier dangled from the ceiling.

'Are you him?' A pair of cream shoes emerged from the darkness at the far end of the hallway. Hawkins shuffled uneasily. Kevin watched warily as the shoes and their owner crossed towards him. There was something precise and unnerving about the way the shoes stood only on the black tiles and never on the white. The clicking of the steps echoed around the gallery. A man emerged into the light. He was tall and skinny, wore a black pinstriped suit and carried a clipboard under one arm. His face remained hidden in shadow. The shoes stopped.

'Name?' The man's Adam's apple bobbed up and down in his long skinny neck.

'Kevin.'

'What did you say, boy?' The apple bobbed again.

'Kevin, sir.'

'Last name?'

'I don't know, sir.'

'Don't know?'

'I was never allowed to know because of my father's job. It was secret, sir.'

'Secret? Your name was *secret*?' The man sounded vaguely amused.

'Not my name, sir; my father's job.'

'A boy who doesn't know his name because it's secret! Ha! And I thought the pupils *here* were stupid!'

'Not my name, sir; it was my father's job that was secret. And because we were always travelling I was given lots of names and I never knew which...'

'Silence!'

The man lifted the clipboard. 'Your notes indicate that your mother and grandparents are all dead and that your father has *disappeared*... Explain!'

'He's working for the Government, overseas, sir.'

'Oh, you mean he's dead!'

'No! Not dead! It's just that I haven't seen him for a year. But I know he's still alive, he...'

'Dead,' concluded the man. 'And like all the other miserable wretches in this place that the Government doesn't know what to do with, you've been given to me!' He sighed and scribbled something on the clipboard. The scribbling suddenly stopped. 'You're dripping on my floor.'

Kevin looked at the puddles around his feet.

'I suggest you get on your knees and lick that mess up.'

Kevin cast a sideways glance at Hawkins who had finished locking the front door and was playing with the key nervously. Lick them up? Surely the man was joking and would laugh at any moment.

The shoes took a pace closer. The man lowered his head, allowing Kevin to see his face for the first time. 'Do you think I'm joking?' The man's greased black hair was parted immaculately to one side. His nose was long and thin like the rest of him, but most unsettling were the eyes. They were cruel and looked in different directions and twitched disturbingly.

'I suggest you do exactly what I tell you.'

Kevin caught Hawkins nodding out the corner of his eye. He was being humiliated, but what else could he do? The cream shoes walked around him. He dropped to his knees and leant down, but as he did, he was kicked forwards across the floor, scraping his chin along the tiles.

'Welcome to school,' exclaimed the man, wiping his shoe on the back of his opposite trouser leg. 'Welcome to the School of Unwanted Children!'

Kevin lifted his chin slowly. It was hurting, but not as much his pride. The tall figure laughed and shot out a hand to Hawkins, 'Key!'

Hawkins offered up the key, which was snatched from him. 'I suggest you show the new boy to his dormitory, Hawkins, before he gets himself into *more* trouble!' With that, the man turned and walked quickly from the hall. Kevin allowed the footsteps to fade away before slowly sitting up.

'Are you, OK?'

A girl was looking at Kevin from the gallery above. He wondered if she'd seen everything.

'I guess!' Kevin blushed and felt his chin, glad to discover it wasn't bleeding.

'That was Mr East!' Hawkins helped Kevin up and handed him his bag. 'Don't worry! He picks on everyone. Did you see his glass eye? Can't miss it, can you? Sometimes, when he leaves the room, he pops it out and leaves it on his desk and says, "I'll be keepin' an eye on you - so behave!" He even leaves it lyin' around school ... so you can never be sure when or where he's watchin' you!'

'Stop it, Spotty!' The girl had appeared next to Kevin. She had a round face, an oriental complexion and a big smile. 'You're scaring him!'

'Mr East isn't in charge,' continued Hawkins, ignoring the girl. 'He's not the head teacher, that's Mrs Waterfield, but she's away ... they say she's got the squits or somethin'... which isn't good! Not the squits, I mean, her being away. Not gone forever, but away. To

18

visit her mum, I think. Actually, I think it's her mum who's got the squits and Mrs Waterfield's gone to visit her. Or perhaps they've both got the squits? Look, I don't know who's got the squits, but Mrs Waterfield is away and that means Mr East is in charge, which isn't good! ... You must be the new boy ... I'm Spotty by the way, Spotty Hawkins, and I know I'm spotty but please don't stare! Pleased to meet you!'

'Pleased to meet you, too!' said Kevin, beginning to feel better and shaking Spotty's hand.

'Spotty likes to talk!' smiled the girl.

'And Cheesy likes to smile!' interrupted Spotty. 'Her real name's Louisy, but we call her Cheesy Louisy. She's from Korea and she likes chocolate and smiling, don't you, Cheesy?'

Cheesy gave Kevin an even bigger smile.

Perhaps Greystones wasn't going to be so bad after all.

Chapter 3

The Three Rules

'This is the courtyard,' explained Cheesy. 'The courtyard is in the middle of the school, so to help you get your bearings, we'll start here. Everyone calls it "the Quad".'

Kevin looked at the tall black windows, which stared down at him from all four sides. The Quad was made of paving stones, most of them cracked. It had a single bench on one side and a single tree on the other. Right in the middle was a waterless pond, and in the middle of the pond was a headless statue.

'That's Dr Greystone,' explained Spotty. 'He was the founder of the school ... which probably explains why his head's gone missin'. It was last seen hangin' from the church bell ... not his real one, the statue's. Mrs Waterfield got right annoyed and we all got detentions. She keeps the head in her office now, on the bookshelf, but she never found out who took it and hung it on the bell. It was pretty obvious though!'

'Who was it?' asked Kevin.

'Lawrence, of course,' said Cheesy. 'Here, let's sit on the bench while we explain a few rules to you. That's it. Squeeze on. Put the bag there, Spotty, and you sit on the other side of Kevin.'

'OK, now in reverse order, rule number three at Greystones is to stay out the way of Mr East.'

'Yeah, I think he's got that one, Cheesy!'

'OK, so rule number two is to stay out the way of Lawrence.'

Kevin looked at the tree on the other side of the Quad, the only one in the school, and wondered if the bench had been specially positioned so pupils could admire it.

'Lawrence Pudding-Pig to be exact,' said Cheesy. 'And if you think Mr East is horrid, Lawrence is *really* horrid. He's as horrid as his name!'

'Yes!' said Spotty, eager to explain. 'He's a right pig! If there's something he can burn, he'll burn it. If there's something he can kick, he'll kick it, and if there's something he can spit on, he'll spit on it. If you ask him how he is, he'll tell you to "stuff it", and if you tell him to "stuff it" he'll kick you where it hurts. And when his mum visits, he slams the car-door in her face and walks off laughin'!'

Kevin lifted his eyebrows. 'How would I recognize him?'

'He's got this big, fake, gold chain,' explained Cheesy.

'Which he stole,' clarified Spotty.

'And he thinks it makes girls fancy him,' Cheesy shuddered.

'Is he big?'

'No, he's scrawny ... but he's nasty. Really nasty.'

'Like a plate of cold vomit,' explained Spotty.

'But if he's so scrawny, then why's everyone scared of him?'

'Because of his gang: Sarah Jones and Tag Short,' said Cheesy. 'She's tall and he's fat. They do what he says. They're tough, but not clever. It's like they share a brain cell between them.'

'And you never know which one's usin' it!' laughed Spotty.

'Where are they now?' asked Kevin, looking up at the windows.

'In lessons, like everyone else, which is why it's so quiet. I'm allowed out to show you around and Cheesy's supposed to be ill, but everyone else is in lessons. There are forty-two of us and we've got the run of the whole building, which is massive, but we're never allowed out. Not in term time anyway. I can't wait for holidays. That's if my uncle's around ... and if he feels like havin' me home.' Spotty stopped and bit his lip. There was an awkward pause before Cheesy changed the subject.

'So why are you here, Kevin? Did you say your dad had disappeared?'

Kevin wriggled his feet uncomfortably. His father had been missing for over a year - a very long year. He hoped he was still alive, but he had no proof. He missed his big hugs and the fun times, like when they'd gone sailing in Italy and when his father had taught him to scuba dive. Life with his father had always been an adventure, but Kevin had never known what job he did. It had all been top secret.

'He gave me this before he disappeared,' explained Kevin, showing them the watch on his right wrist. 'He said it would help me if anything ever happened to me.'

'Totally cool!' whistled Spotty, looking at the chrome face with all the buttons. 'How's it work?'

'I don't know!' replied Kevin sheepishly. 'Sometimes it lights up or

I see numbers or letters, but I can never understand them ... and that's not all.' He unbuckled the strap and turned the watch over. 'There's a photo stuck on the back and I've no idea who it is.'

Cheesy and Spotty bent closer. The woman's face was old and wrinkled. Her sharp features and thin chin made her look quite mean. Spotty sat back up and whistled again. 'A mystery! Wow!'

'Yes, a mystery,' said Kevin, buckling the strap back on. 'Just like the leaning turret.'

Cheesy and Spotty looked at one another.

'What?'

'Nothing,' said Cheesy jumping up from the bench. 'Come on, we'll show you to your dormitory. There are five boy dorms and four girl dorms. The boys are on the second floor, the girls are on the third. That wing over there leads to the offices, that one to the dining room and that one to the science classrooms.'

'And the leaning turret,' added Kevin.

'Look,' said Cheesy firmly, 'I don't really want to talk about it, but just so you know, just so we can say that we warned you, rule number one at Greystones is: Never, ever, go into the Forbidden Turret.'

Chapter 4

Spooky Stories

'I don't understand. How can you be so scared of a turret?' Kevin shrugged and continued to unpack. 'I know it's got a history, but surely they're just stories.'

'True stories,' said Spotty stubbornly. He was sitting on the end of Kevin's bed, hugging his knees. 'They scare Cheesy. That's why she left to go to her dorm. She doesn't like talkin' about them.'

'But even if they are true, they're history.'

'History that keeps happenin'! And it's not just the stories, it's all the other stuff.'

'What stuff?'

Spotty shook his head. For once he didn't want to talk.

Kevin folded his last shirt and shut the drawer. He sat down on his pillow and crossed his legs. 'What stuff? You can tell me. I am sharing a bunk with you.'

'OK!' Spotty said suddenly. 'It's all the weird stuff that happens here. It's always to do with the turret. It's what happens at night. Not every night, but sometimes. Lights. We've all seen them. Green glowing lights. Then there was the crack that ran down the wall. All the way down. We watched it. We thought the turret was falling, but then it closed back up again, all on its own, as good as new. There was the monkey and the boy that disappeared last year and ...'

'Whoa!' said Kevin holding up both hands. 'Slow down!'

But Spotty wasn't slowing for anyone. His eyes had grown large and he was talking as if his life depended on it. 'Miss Teeling, she saw the monkey first. It just walked into her classroom. But it wasn't a normal monkey. It was huge ... and it spoke! I heard it. It apologized! Said it was looking for someone and then shut the door and went out. We all followed it with our rulers and chairs .... the whole class. We followed it to the turret and trapped it. We locked it in. Miss Teeling, she called for help, but when they went up, there was nothing there - apart from the box!' Spotty stared ahead of him as if Kevin wasn't there. 'It's not the turret, you know. It's the box. It's always the box. They never find anything else. Just the box.'

'What box?'

'Would you like to find out?' A new voice spoke from the door. Kevin had been so engrossed in what Spotty was saying that he hadn't realised anyone else had come into the room. A second boy followed the first and they crossed to where Kevin and Spotty were sitting. The first boy bent over and stared at Kevin. He had pale skin, untidy brown hair and a large golden chain that dangled from his neck.

'Someone new!' The boy straightened up, but as he did, his scrawny arm shot into Kevin's stomach, winding him.

'Ugly too! Orange hair and spots all over.'

'Aren't they freckles, Lawrence?' said the second boy in a nasally voice.

'No Tag, they're tiny spots!' said the first, spitting in Kevin's face. 'I hate new boys especially ugly ones like you!'

Kevin gasped as another punch landed in his stomach, making him double up. This wasn't the first time he'd been bullied. It had happened to him in previous schools - and always because of his hair. Once he'd even missed school because he couldn't bear the thought of being picked on. Everyone thought it was so original and funny, but they didn't know how it felt.

'New boys have to be *initiated*!' Tag laughed, holding Spotty back with a firm arm. 'Locked in the turret!'

'With the box!' added Lawrence in a spooky voice. 'Mind you, being *new*, he doesn't know anything about that!'

Lawrence licked his scabby lips and leant into Kevin's face. 'You see, over the years, there have been disappearances. People have gone missing. Poof! Vanished! There was this boy ... a new boy ... just like you - but not as ugly ... We locked him in the turret with the box one stormy night. Oh! You should have heard the screams! And in the morning there was silence ... *deathly silence*!' Lawrence bent even closer. 'And when the teachers finally managed to get the door open, all they found was his left shoe ... with his foot still in it!'

Lawrence laughed at the horrified look on Kevin's face. He pushed Kevin back and straightened up. 'So, we'll see you tonight then!' Lawrence glared at Spotty and beckoned to Tag to follow. He paused at the door before turning to Kevin. 'And don't forget to wear your shoes!'

Kevin gulped as the door closed.

'Ignore them!' reassured Spotty, breathing a long sigh of relief. 'They won't come.'

But, of course, they did.

Chapter 5

In the Forbidden Turret

'No teacher will look for you up here!' nodded Lawrence, pushing Kevin into the middle of the turret floor. 'Or if they do there won't be *much* of you left to find!' Kevin heard the heavy door slam behind him and the sound of a key being turned.

Then silence.

He spat out the old sock and shivered, glad he hadn't undressed to go to bed that night. Old rafters, held in place by a couple of recently nailed planks, criss-crossed upwards into the pointed roof. The sloping walls were cold and grey and were covered in small holes, a perfect haunt for bats and spiders. He'd expected the room to be filled with all types of bric-a-brac and rubbish, but it was empty. Empty, except for an object lit by a shaft of moonlight coming from a skylight in the roof.

It was a box.

Another surge of panic rose inside him and he took a wary step backwards. The box wasn't much to look at. It had no fancy carvings; it was just a blue box with a keyhole.

A sudden *beep* from his watch made him jump. He glanced at his wrist and for one brief moment he thought he saw words. He'd never seen that before. Was it a warning? Even more alert, Kevin stared suspiciously at the box.

Should he open it? Surely all those stories had been lies, invented

to frighten new boys like him? So what if something happened to him? No one would care; no one would even notice. He was just a new kid with orange hair and freckles - or spots, that's what Lawrence had called them - stuck in a school for unwanted children.

He looked at the box again. The sensible part of him wanted to leave it well alone, but the other part was curious. What was in the box? Why was everyone afraid of it? Second-by-second and bit-by-bit, with trembling hands, he reached forward. The floorboard beneath him creaked in anticipation. Nearer and nearer he stretched. A few more centimetres, a few more seconds, and he would know. His insides shrieked with fear as he touched the lid. Carefully, slowly, he went to lift it up ... it was locked. *Locked*!

A flood of disappointment swept over him. So this was what all those horror stories were about: a pathetic locked box.

As he turned away a long, drawn-out wail sliced the night air, freezing him to the spot. A black shadow flew across the wall. Shining eyes stared at him. He relaxed as he saw what it was - a small, black cat hiding in the shadows. The cat gave a loud meow, hopped gracefully onto the box, up to a ledge on the wall and through the skylight into the night beyond. Kevin frowned. If the cat could get out, perhaps he could too.

Clambering onto the box, he strained to reach the ledge. All of a sudden, the box wobbled. Kevin's eyes widened as it slipped from beneath him. With a shocked cry and a frantic lunge, he clawed desperately at the ledge and as he did, his fingers closed around something cold and hard. Tumbling backwards, arms flailing, he crashed to the ground.

He rolled onto his back and breathed a sigh of relief that he wasn't badly hurt. Rubbing his elbow, he held up his new find so that it glinted in the moonlight. A key. Would it unlock the door? An excited tingling crept across his back. Maybe it was for the box?

But then something unbelievable started to happen. The key started to *bend*. It twisted in his fingers, first one way and then the other. He tried to throw it away, but couldn't - it was stuck firmly to his hand!

And then, quite suddenly, the key gave such a jerk that Kevin's whole arm was yanked forwards, forcing him to sit up. A second jerk pulled him to his feet and another one forced him to step forward, making him realise something terrifying: the key was pulling him towards the box.

The box had begun to tremble. Kevin could see the keyhole glowing, bathing him and the room in an eerie green light. Step by step, the key tugged him across the floor. Struggling frantically, he tried to prise the key free, but it was no use. With each tug, it pulled him closer.

Suddenly, Kevin remembered the horror stories and his heart began to pound. Was this what had happened to the other missing people? Desperately he kicked upwards, ripping the key from his hand, sending it spinning until it suddenly stopped in mid-air, hovering centimetres from his face. Kevin swallowed, his mouth went dry and an uncontrollable shiver ran down his spine. It was unbelievable! A key was hovering in mid air. A law of physics was being broken right before his eyes.

Very slowly and purposefully, the key turned to face the box. Like a missile, it flew forward and slammed into the box's keyhole.

And the moment it did, everything stopped. The box sat silent; the key stuck lifeless in the lock; the light went out; the room was still. All Kevin could hear was his heart pounding. The seconds ticked by, minutes passed, but still nothing happened. Eventually, he let out a long silent sigh of relief and took a step back, trying to reason what had happened. Had someone been playing a game with him, a practical joke? He knew they hadn't. It was something else. Something he didn't understand.

'It's not the turret, you know, it's the box.' He remembered Spotty's words. 'It's always the box.'

What secret did the box hold? What mystery lay inside? What would happen if he looked? He hurriedly dismissed the last thought - it would be a stupid thing to do, especially after what had just happened.

He walked around the room. There was no escape through the door and no chance of getting to the skylight without standing on the box.

Spotty's words echoed round Kevin's head. 'The box, always the box.' He tried to gather his thoughts together as best he could. What did he have to lose if he looked? He didn't have a future. All he wanted was to see his father again and there wasn't much hope of that. He paced around the room until he couldn't contain his curiosity any longer. In two quick strides he reached the box, turned the key and lifted the lid.

And that's when it happened.

Chapter 6
The Underground Cave

Deep, deep, deep underground in another world, was a cave.

'Oh, lovely ... lovely ... lovely!' hissed the voice.

The cave was lit with green and red candles that sent long shadows flickering across its polished stone table and hard slate floor. A long black poker hung from the crooked shelf above the lifeless fireplace, in front of which sat an empty, battered armchair. A tin lantern dangled from a white, knobbly root that protruded from a crack in the low roof. The tip of the root moved slowly back and forth, as if thriving off some unseen energy. Tiny cave bugs crawled across the walls, each giving off a green glow as they munched on luminescent button mushrooms that grew from the cracks and crevices.

'Lovely!' The voice seemed pleased. The candles danced excitedly in response, causing a large warty toad to retreat further into the dark.

'Plob! Where are you? *Plob*!'

A balding dwarf with a dripping nose and clothed in brown cloth hurried from another cave.

'Yeth, mathter. I am here. What ith it?' Plob didn't have many teeth left and speaking wasn't easy.

'Oh, I do wish you'd learn to talk properly, Plob!' said the voice. 'Stop spitting all over my cave and fetch me my spell book.'

Plob's small brown eyes filled with fear and he paused just long enough for the speaker to notice.

'What's wrong, Plob? ... Are you *afraid*?'

'No! No, mathter,' said the dwarf, who clearly *was* afraid. He scurried into the shadows and re-emerged with a green, knobbly, hardback book.

'Put it here, Plob.'

Plob carefully sidestepped the half-chewed remains of a squashed frog, but failed to notice a warthog's eyeball that was being rolled across the floor by a pair of dung beetles. The dwarf cried with alarm as his foot slipped and the book was sent sailing high into the air, landing with a loud squelch in a bowl of jellyfish.

'Fool!' screamed his master.

Plob hurriedly picked himself up, carefully fished out the book and pushed it onto the stone table. He shuffled backwards, slipped on the eyeball once more and turned to leave when the voice spoke again.

'Don't leave Plob ... I may need you!'

Plob froze. Every inch of his body was shaking with fear: a fear that had held him captive for three hundred and seventy five long years, a fear that was controlled by the shrivelled, hunched figure at the table. Fortunately the figure was shrouded in a black cloak,

protecting him from the glare of its evil eyes. It was muttering. Plob could make out occasional words.

'Interesting ... interesting ... another one has found a way into my world ... hmm .... What should I do? Send a present? No ... even better, I should welcome them *personally*.' The cloaked figure cackled and looked at the shelf in front with its multitude of jars, specimens and plants. There was a jar of warthog eyes (with one missing), a box of bat wings in chilli sauce, powdered old women's warts and a giant jar of dinosaur dung complete with live writhing maggots.

The sorcerer mumbled something before consulting his spell book.

'Oh, tut tut! It appears that I *do* need your help after all, Plob!'

'Mathter ... I ... I ... How do you mean?'

'Children! You know how I *love* them! I feel it is time to add another one to my ... Collection! Hmm ... I seem to have most of the ingredients I need to make the spell ... except one, that is. I seem to have run out of teeth again!'

A thin yellow arm snaked out from the cloak. It had only a stub of a hand with a large claw attached.

The claw beckoned to Plob.

Chapter 7
The Library of Knowledge

It had happened fast. One moment Kevin was lifting the lid, the next he had fallen into the box. The blackness changed into a green swirling tunnel and a blast of wind slapped him in the face, preventing him from screaming. The wind pulled at his face and clothes, tugging him further down the twisting tunnel. But then, as quickly as it had started, it was over and he was left lying face down.

Kevin blinked. His cheek and nose were pressed uncomfortably against a wooden floor. He flexed his arms and wriggled his toes. Apart from his bruised stomach, where Lawrence had punched him, he didn't hurt at all - he was completely unharmed.

Lifting his head, he gazed around. Aisles and aisles of bookcases surrounded him, crammed with every shape of book imaginable: tall ones, skinny ones, fat ones, blue books, red books, hard-back, leather-bound, loose pages and magazines jammed into every available space. Oversized books were piled on a sagging library cart, blocking the aisle ahead, while several piles reached all the way to the ceiling. The whole place smelt

musty and old and for a moment he wondered whether he'd fallen through the bottom of the box into part of the school. He'd never seen so many books.

But there was something else. Watching him, from behind two

 piles of books, was a strange-looking creature. It had crazy orange hair, a squashed face, and eyebrows and ears that stuck out in an ugly manner, as if they'd been pushed onto its head as an afterthought. Kevin sat up warily. The creature did the same. Kevin got to his feet. The creature copied him. Kevin suddenly realised something dreadful: the creature wasn't copying him - it *was* him.

Trembling, he approached the mirror in disbelief and tapped the glass. His face was so ... *strange*! He scrunched his eyebrows, wiggled his ears and licked his nose. Everything felt the same, but it wasn't. He turned his hands over and gazed in horror at his new chubby fingers. His stomach filled with dread as he imagined how he'd get picked on now. He'd thought he was ugly before, but this was worse. He gave a little sniff. What had the box done to him?

'Oh! It's still not working!' said a voice nearby, making Kevin jump. 'Work! Work! Work! Oh, come on!' Kevin dropped to the floor and dived behind a long red settee, not wanting to be seen looking the way he was.

'What's wrong with it? Why won't it send?' The voice sounded cross. 'It's this library! This stupid library ... Oh! Hang on! ... Yes, I've got a signal!'

The voice belonged to a girl and was coming from the opposite side of the bookcase. Checking no one else was around, Kevin quietly slid the trolley to one side. He shuffled forward, nose to the ground.

'... Oh, it's *still* not working! ... It's this library! I know it is! It won't let me send texts and it won't let me out!'

Whoever the girl was seemed to be as lost as he was. He peered around the base of the bookcase. She was sitting in a red leather chair a few yards in front of him, holding a mobile phone.

'Aaaaaaaaaaaaaah!' the girl screamed as she saw Kevin. 'Who ... I mean ... *what* are you?' She was about his age, perhaps a year or two older, with attractive green eyes and red cheeks. Her plum-coloured hair was tied in bunches and she was dressed in a grey school uniform with a red-striped tie. 'Well, whatever you are,' said the girl jumping to her feet, 'I demand you get me out of here, *now*!'

Kevin stood up, still hiding behind the bookcase.

The girl eyed him suspiciously. 'You look weird! ... Sorry!!' she added, seeing Kevin's hurt expression, 'I don't mean to be rude, but you do. You look all rubbery and like a monkey ... Oh, I shouldn't really say it like that ... I'm sorry.'

'I don't normally look like this!' blurted Kevin. 'I've just got here. It's this place. It's done something weird to me.'

'Made you look like that?' said the girl, feeling sorry for Kevin. 'What, changed the way you look?' She shuddered. 'I knew it! This library *is* magic. I've tried to find a way out, but I can't. I was in my bedroom doing my homework and then suddenly I was here! Sounds spooky, doesn't it? Well it is. Totally ... Oh!' The girl stood up excitedly. She was a couple of inches taller than Kevin. 'Your watch! Can I try texting your watch - to see if my phone's working?'

'Sure!' agreed Kevin, holding out his hand. 'I don't know if it receives texts, though.'

'Don't know how your watch works?' frowned the girl. 'That's pretty dumb, isn't it?'

Kevin was just opening his mouth to reply, when his watch gave an extra loud beep and a long number appeared on the screen.

'Oh!' said the girl, surprised. 'Well, your watch seems to understand!' She copied the number into her phone. 'I'm Misty by the way, who are you?'

'Kevin,' said Kevin, looking at his watch, dumfounded. He was just about to explain how his watch seemed to have a mind of its own, when a large hairy hand appeared before his eyes. Long brown fingers entwined themselves around his collar and hauled him upwards in a wide arc. The hand dumped him into a battered floral armchair, jammed between the rafters, several metres above where he'd been standing.

Kevin gave a cry of shock as Misty was dropped into his lap, causing two springs to ping energetically from the side of the chair. Opening his mouth to complain, he promptly shut it as he caught sight of the owner of the hairy hand.

A long maroon snout protruded from between a pair of penetrating eyes. The face was framed by two flaps of sky-blue skin and topped with an explosion of wild hair. It was a giant monkey!

'Shhhhhhhhhh!' hushed the monkey, sternly raising a finger to his lips. He swayed back and forth from a metal ring in the ceiling. 'No gabbing in the Library!'

'Oh!' exclaimed Misty. 'A talking monkey!'

The monkey looked behind him, confused, before realizing that Misty was actually talking about *him*. He looked delightedly at Misty. 'I can read too, which is helpful as I look after the books.'

Kevin was stunned. He'd never seen such a big monkey and he'd certainly never heard one *talk*.

'Do you know where we are?' asked Misty.

The monkey heaved out his chest in obvious delight. 'Where? Where? Of course I do! You're in the Library of Knowledge, the centre of *everything*!' The monkey hooted with laughter and somersaulted onto a nearby rafter. 'I'm not really Australian,' he laughed, 'I may sound Aussie, but I'm not. Naaaaa! It's just that one day a geography book flipped open and before I knew it … Whoa! There I was, stuck in a cage in Sydney Zoo!'

'Stuck in the book?' said Misty, confused.

'Fortunately someone saw me and pulled me out!'

'You fell *into* the book?' exclaimed Misty. 'Is that how I got here? Through a book?'

'Hmm! I thought we'd collected all the books,' said the monkey to himself, 'but maybe there are a few still left in your world that we haven't found yet.'

'We're in another world?' Kevin interrupted. 'Is that why I look like this?'

The monkey eyed him strangely. 'Like what? You look alright to me.'

Kevin scrunched his face and wiggled his fingers. 'I don't usually look like this!'

The monkey gave a little whistle. 'You must be special! People don't normally change when they come here!'

'But I have!'

'Hold on!' Misty was still puzzled. 'How can a book bring me here? Books don't do that!'

'Whoa!' The monkey held up his hand. 'You don't understand!' He leant forward and whispered with his big lips. 'These books can take you *anywhere*! The Library of Knowledge is the centre of all the worlds.'

Kevin frowned. 'Worlds?'

The monkey looked over his shoulder, before giving them a wink. 'Do you want me to show you?' Not waiting for a reply, he dropped to the floor and pointed to a downward ladder. 'Come on!'

Kevin and Misty looked at each other. They didn't have much choice. Cautiously they shuffled along the rafter and down the stepladder.

'The name's Martin and I work here,' said the monkey helping them down the last few rungs. 'I'm a mandrill, that's a sort of baboon. Now follow me and be quiet. We don't want Randolph knowing you're here.'

'Randolph?' said Misty. 'Who's he? Does he work here too?'

'Randolph's the boss ... and we sure respect him! He lives here - we all do. Everyone knows that monkeys look after the Library.'

'Who's that?'

Martin followed Kevin's pointing finger. An ape was pushing a ladder on castor wheels towards them. With a gasp Martin dragged them back around the corner. 'It's Randolph!' he whispered, beginning to panic. 'Go that way! No ... this way ... Wait! He'll *kill* me if he catches you here. I'll be in such trouble. He'll halve my banana allowance or ban me from having Friday's Chocolate Mousse Surprise.' Martin looked deeply distressed. Friday's Chocolate Mousse Surprise was obviously not to be missed. 'He doesn't allow visitors in this part of the libr ... aaaah! ... Randolph!'

A gibbon blocked their path. Round glasses ringed a knowing pair of eyes. His grey hair was parted perfectly in the middle and a large golden pocket watch dangled from a chain that swung from his neck. Randolph's brown eyes passed from the mandrill to the children and back to the mandrill. 'Martin? An explanation if you please?'

'I ... err ... you see ... err ... last week ... um ... no!' gulped Martin.

Randolph frowned. 'We don't allow visitors, do we, Martin?' said the gibbon sternly, raising an eyebrow.

'No!' replied Martin, lowering his head in shame.

'And we know what happens to monkeys that disobey the Library rules, don't we, Martin?'

'Yes,' sniffed Martin, not bothering to look up.

'No!' Misty interrupted, trying to defend Martin, 'Wait! You don't understand...'

'SILENCE IN THE LIBRARY!' barked the gibbon, making everyone jump. Randolph extended his extraordinarily long arms and clasped both hands together in front of his lips with the first fingers pointing upwards. 'Silence in the Library!' he repeated, this time in a whisper.

'But we're here by accident!' whispered back Misty.

'Through a box,' said Kevin.

'And a book,' added Misty.

Randolph gave Kevin a long stare over the top of his glasses. 'Did you say *box*?'

Kevin nodded.

'Oh dear! Not again. That box has proved quite a handful over the years - people getting in when they shouldn't.'

'A boy got in last year,' added Martin, 'but before we could help him he opened one of the books. We never did find him - apart from his foot - but we put that back.'

'Martin, please!' said Randolph sternly.

'The box brought me here?' said Kevin, trying to understand.

'Sort of,' agreed Randolph. 'It's got a mind of its own though - sometimes it works and sometimes it doesn't, but I was told to leave it there in the school, so that an orange-haired boy can one day ... find it. Oh!'

Kevin looked at Randolph, wondering why the gibbon had stopped talking. Randolph was staring at his hair. Everyone was staring at his hair.

Randolph removed his glasses, rubbed them, put them back on and stared again. 'It's you! You're him. You're the one!' The gibbon gave an excited whoop and then an apologetic cough. 'Change of plan,' he cried, turning and leaping onto a bookcase. 'Follow me! Martin, you too. Quickly now!'

'What? Up there?' said Misty.

'Naaa! Along the ground with me,' beamed Martin, pleased not to be in trouble anymore. 'Come on! You've got him excited and Randolph never gets excited. Hurry!'

'I don't understand,' said Kevin, running after Martin. 'What does he mean, "I'm the one"?'

'All will be explained!' said Martin, clearly delighted with the opportunity to run in the Library. 'This way! Just don't touch the books!'

'Why not?' questioned Kevin.

"Cause they're magic!' said Martin over his shoulder. 'Pick one up, open its pages and ... Whoosh! You fall in!' He looked at Misty.

'That's what happened to you. You found one of our books in your world. Not knowing what it was, you touched its pages and were instantly transported here!'

'What's in them all?' asked Kevin, carefully avoiding a pile of books.

'Different things!' Martin waved to a hanging baby orang-utan who, by the look on its face, had never seen anyone running in the Library before. 'There are History books - they're mostly about people, Geography books - they contain thousands of worlds like the one you came from, Reference books, Science books ...'

'Other worlds?' interrupted Misty.

'Yes! And the Geography section is where they're kept.' Martin stopped and opened his arms wide. 'You can travel anywhere! You've never lived if you've not visited the Washoloff Swamps with their singing octopus!' Martin shook his head at their bewildered looks. 'My favourite is the world of Giant Laughing Ants. Ha! Now they'd make you laugh!' He turned and bounded away. 'Come on! We can't stand here talking. We'll lose Randolph. This way!'

They ran down the aisle, catching a glimpse of Randolph leaping between bookcases ahead of them. The Library seemed endless. They passed through a pair of tall doors into a grand reading room. The walls were decorated with paintings of stern-looking monkeys who glared down at them.

'Past head librarians,' chuckled Martin, bounding across the room. 'I don't think they like us running in their library!' He pointed to rows of leather-bound books. 'These are the History books - written in permanent ink. We can't change them. They're recorded forever. But the Future books ... now they're a different matter! No one's allowed in *that* section. The gorillas look after them. High security, you see. We'd all like to know what happens in the future, wouldn't we?' They exited the room through more double-doors.

'It's rumoured that all the pages in the Future books are blank, so that people can write their own futures themselves,' continued Martin. 'But some say the Future books are already written with invisible ink and when you start to live your life, it's only then that the writing appears - as if your future has already been written for you.'

'Wow!' panted Misty, beginning to get out of breath, 'I hope it happens the first way. I want to write my own future! Where is the Future section anyway?'

'In the Top Secret section!'

'Where's that?' puffed Kevin.

> **'Wow!' panted Misty, '... I want to write my own future!'**

'By the Black books. No one touches them. That's where evil lives.'

'Black books?' said Kevin, 'Where are they?'

'Next to the Future books!' explained Martin.

'But where are *they*?' asked Misty, getting exasperated.

'Mostly in the Top Secret section!' Martin came sliding to a halt beside Randolph.

'Which is *where*?' said Kevin and Misty together.

'Here!' said Martin, gazing up at a pair of solid steel gates. 'Right *here*!'

'TOP SECRET,' said the sign on the gates. 'KEEP OUT! TOP SECRET.'

And then in big red letters underneath ...

'DANGER!'

Chapter 8
Into the Future

There was a thudding CRUNCH as something monstrous moved behind the gates.

CRUNCH! Another heavy footstep.

CRUNCH! A small panel in the door slid open, revealing a dark face. Misty gulped and took a step back as the probing eyes stared into hers. It was a gorilla, a very *big* gorilla.

'Who goes there?' piped the giant ape in a voice so high-pitched that Kevin would have laughed if it hadn't looked so scary. 'Friend or foe?'

'Me!' said Randolph.

'*Who*?' squeaked the gorilla.

'Randolph!'

'Who?' said the gorilla, squinting at the gibbon.

'Gorillas have bad memories!' explained Martin out the corner of his mouth. 'The larger they get, the worse their memories become!'

'Oh!' whispered Misty, learning something new about gorillas.

'Me!' barked Randolph tapping his foot impatiently. There was the sound of a bar being lifted before the gates were swung open, allowing them to pass through.

'Wow!' said Misty, looking around. She hadn't expected the Top Secret section to look so enormous. The bookcases were made of stainless steel and were arranged in perfect lines. They were illuminated by hundreds of spotlights built into the upper shelves. The bookcases seemed to go on forever, reaching thousands of shelves high and stretching as far as she could see.

'Look!' said Misty, pointing directly upwards. 'I think it's a bridge.' Kevin could see a walkway high above them joining two bookcases. A small dot with a tail was walking across.

'This way!' said Randolph. They stayed close to Martin as they passed the gorilla whose watchful eyes followed their every step. A second gorilla sat silently amongst the books, with his hand across his mouth. Kevin felt sure the gorilla was laughing at his hair and thinking how ugly he was.

'TOP SECRET,' said a sign, reminding them of where they were.

'Climb on!' said Randolph, pointing to a round metal plate on the floor. The plate was a couple of metres wide, had a central pole a metre high, and a handrail all around. They stepped up beside Randolph and watched as Martin clicked the final piece of handrail into place behind them. There was a faint humming noise and a slight jolt that made their knees buckle slightly. The plate rose into the air and, after only a few seconds, came to a gentle stop. Kevin leant over the edge and ʼ ᴏcked at how high they'd climbed. Martin waved up at hⁱ   ᵘⁱck wave back before hastily moving to the ·

grabbing the central pole. He watched

moved his hand through the air, makⁱ

appear. The screen flickered and hummed with energy as Randolph tapped on it with his fingers.

'Now, let's see!' Randolph looked at Misty. 'Name?'

'Misty.'

'There are thousands of Mistys,' said Randolph. 'Full name?'

'Misty J. Gilmore.'

Randolph tapped on the screen again, before smiling triumphantly. 'Ah! There you are! Aisle 79, Shelf 712, Book 320 ... that was easy!' He turned off the screen and reached for the rail. 'I'd hold on if I were you,' he added.

There was a humming noise before the machine shot sideways, knocking Kevin and Misty to the floor. They grabbed the central pole and held on, terrified, as they flew at a terrific speed between the bookcases. They were travelling so fast they couldn't speak. Kevin could feel the wind tearing at his hair. The machine came to a jarring halt, causing their bodies to slide around the floor, turning like two hands on a clock face. But the machine wasn't finished. It flew violently upwards, making their stomachs lurch, and then sideways again, before coming to another sudden stop.

'We're here!' said Randolph, ignoring their pale faces.

'You could have warned us!' said Misty, breathing hard.

'I did,' said Randolph, leaning over the edge of the rail. Kevin sat up. The machine was parked several thousand feet in the air and was hovering between two bookcases that were full of millions of tical hard-back yellow books. He watched Randolph running his fingers across the spines.

'... 317 ... 318 ... 319 ... 320 ... here it is!' The gibbon pulled a book from the shelf and peered at its cover. He looked at Misty and back to the book. 'Bobby Gilder? No, that's not right. What's gone wrong? ... Ah, silly me! This is shelf 722!'   Randolph returned the book to the shelf and promptly jumped off the edge of the machine.

'Randolph!' screamed Misty. She turned and stared at Kevin. 'He just jumped!' Kevin scrambled to the edge, making the machine tilt. Randolph was hanging by one arm from a shelf a few metres below. He appeared to be rummaging through a row of books, not at all bothered by the huge drop beneath him.

'I think he's OK!' said Kevin. 'He looks as if he knows what he's doing.' Misty breathed a sigh of relief. She felt even better when, several seconds later, Randolph climbed up the bookcase and back onto the machine, carrying a book. He held it up for Misty to see.

'MISTY J. GILMORE,' said the title.

Misty gasped.

The gibbon held up a hand, 'No questions, not yet.' He looked at Kevin. 'Your turn. Name?'

'Kevin.'

'Kevin what?'

'Just Kevin. It's my only name.'

Randolph frowned. 'You must have another name. Everyone in

your world has more than one name!' He furrowed his brow. 'That doesn't make sense. You have to have a double name to be filed and everyone is filed ... A at the top, Z at the bottom ... I could try and cross reference you, but that still wouldn't make sense ... Aaaaaah! ... The only place you could be is ... yes, I remember now! Ha!' Randolph gave a little jump of glee, making the machine wobble. He pointed at two straps hanging from the central pole. 'I suggest you use the seat belts this time!' He opened a small compartment in the floor and put Misty's book inside. He closed the lid, checked their belts and wrapped his tail around the side rail. 'Now hold on,' he said. 'And don't say I didn't warn you this time!'

The machine gave its warning hum before suddenly flipping upside down. Misty screamed. Kevin closed his eyes and tried not to think about the thin seatbelt that was dangling him thousands of feet in the air.

'I thought you'd like to see where you're going!' said Randolph. 'Here we go!'

Kevin's eyes shot open as the machine dropped like a stone. The floor raced towards them. He braced himself, but at the last second the floor parted and they plunged through into darkness. The machine slowed to a halt, gave another little hum and then flipped back to its upright position.

'Please, can we never do that again?' Kevin heard Misty whimper in the dark next to him.

'It was good, wasn't it?' Randolph didn't seem to have been bothered by their near-death experience one little bit.

A light came on making Kevin blink. They were at the bottom of a long shaft. Around them were a number of brick arches leading into tunnels. He shivered as he looked into the darkness, glad he wasn't on his own. The craft went through the first archway and lights came on one by one as they passed slowly up a brick tunnel. There was only enough light to see just ahead or to either side, but he could make out a maze of tunnels branching off in all directions.

'The Library cellar,' explained Randolph, bringing the machine to a halt and stepping off. He gestured with his arm. 'We keep books that we don't know what to do with down here.'

'It's empty,' said Misty looking around.

'That's because we know what to do with all the books,' said Randolph. He walked to a lone table and picked up something covered in cobwebs. He wiped it with his tail and blew off the dust. 'Except this one! I put it here, now ... it must have been, what? Sixty years ago? ... Phew!' He whistled and climbed aboard, holding the book so they could see the cover in the dim light.

'KEVIN,' said the title.

Kevin was confused. What was a book with his name on doing in a cellar all on its own? Why was it separated from the rest, forgotten and unwanted? It was just like the rest of his life. A tear appeared in the corner of his eye, which he brushed away ashamedly.

'Now,' said Randolph, looking at his pocket watch, 'I suggest I explain everything to you back in the comfort of the Lounge. I expect you're quite hungry, aren't you? ... I thought as much. Have you ever tried Friday's Chocolate Mousse Surprise? ... No? Oh, we'll have to put that right!' He smacked his lips. 'And as this is a special occasion, I think I'll have some too!'

Chapter 9
Why Bullying isn't
a *Trifle*-ing Matter

Meanwhile, back at Greystones School - quite literally a world away - Lawrence Pudding-Pig licked his spotty lips. He could still taste his last mouthful of stolen trifle. The cream had been his favourite, even though he felt a bit sick after having eaten so much. He could just about make out Tag's large shape under the bed covers on the opposite side of the dormitory. He imagined Tag's eyebrows going up and down as he snored - eyebrows that met in the middle, as if someone had painted a thick black line across his forehead. Lawrence liked his two friends, Tag and Sarah - not because he cared about them whatsoever, but because they were useful. They weren't particularly clever - he'd admit that. In fact, they were about as clever as a thick-crusted sandwich without the filling. But Lawrence liked it that way. He could manipulate them to do what he wanted. He clenched his fists with glee under the blankets as he realised that tomorrow was Friday. Friday was the day when they'd bunk school early and descend on the local primary school to bully the little kids. Our Lady of the Parish of St. Augustinian the Third in the Dell Primary School had a ridiculous name, which Lawrence liked because he had such fun spraying graffiti all over its lengthy sign. He got a real kick out of vandalising it because he knew it cost the school so much money to clean and that *he* was responsible for the expense. Lawrence enjoyed bullying the little kids. He especially liked throwing stones at them and making them cry.

He'd liked picking on the new boy too. He could imagine him now in the Forbidden Turret, cold and alone and crying like a pathetic baby.

A new thought dawned on Lawrence: what if he was to take the empty trifle bowl up to the turret? He could leave it there so the new boy got the blame. And if the boy was asleep, he'd give him a good kick to really scare him.

It was an excellent idea and too tempting to ignore. Hopping out of bed he pulled on his clothes and crossed to the door. He thought about waking Tag, but decided not to; he'd keep the glory for himself and tell Tag and Sarah in the morning. Like a silent hyena, Lawrence opened the door, crossed into the hall and padded down the deserted corridor beyond. He kept to the shadows, all the while being careful not to let the trifle bowl bang on the iron radiators. He made his way across the silent school to the Forbidden Turret and stealthily climbed the stairs until he stood before the oak door. He paused to listen, but hearing nothing, he quietly turned the key and peered into the moonlit room. For a moment he was confused - there was no one there - but then he saw the box. The new boy must be sleeping inside.

He smiled at the thought of all the rumours he'd spread concerning the box. Some kids were dumb enough to believe such nonsense. He tiptoed over to it, pausing only for a moment as he saw the key protruding from the lock. He was puzzled as to why he hadn't seen the key there before, but the thought of using it to lock both the trifle bowl and the new boy in the box together overruled all logic. He raised the bowl, ready to slam it down on Kevin. Lawrence laughed and lifted the lid - but the moment he did something happened very fast.

An enormous hand reached out. It grabbed him by the collar and pulled him violently inside the box, so that just his legs were sticking out. Lawrence found himself nose to nose with the biggest gorilla he had ever seen. Its black eyes glared right into his. Its breath was hot on his face and its teeth shone white in the dark. It was the longest second of Lawrence's life. He was petrified. But before he could make a single noise, something grabbed him by the shoulder and hauled him back into the attic room.

'What are you doing?' roared an angry voice. Lawrence stared open-mouthed at the towering figure of Mr East, who suddenly recognized him. 'Pudding-Pig! *What* are you doing stuffing your face into a box at this time of night?'

Lawrence could hardly stand. His knees were knocking and his legs had turned to rubber. 'M ... m ... monkey!' he stammered, pointing at the now empty box. 'Monkey!'

'What?' shouted Mr East, getting even angrier. 'Are you calling me a monkey?' His glass eye twitched madly. 'Do you have the audacity to call *me* a monkey?' He suddenly froze and took a deep breath as he caught sight of the bowl in Lawrence's hand. 'Is that what I think it is, boy?'

Lawrence looked down at the bowl. He was so terrified he hadn't the strength to hold it anymore. It clattered to the floor.

'Pudding-Pig!' Mr East's voice was barely audible between his clenched teeth. 'By the time I have finished with you, you are going to wish you had never, never, been born!'

Lawrence gave a cry of pain as the biology teacher reached forward and twisted his ear, forcing him across the room and down the stairs. Like most bullies when they are bullied themselves, Lawrence began to cry. He wailed and whined and whimpered, yet despite his tears, he knew that he *had* seen a monkey. He also had a definite feeling that it had something to do with the new boy, who would pay with his life if he ever got his hands on him. But then he gave up thinking because the pain in his ear became too much for him as he was dragged, blubbing, all the way back to the dormitories.

Chapter 10
Black Book Confusion

Kevin finished his Friday's Chocolate Mousse Surprise and looked longingly at Misty's bowl. He watched her eat the last few mouthfuls. Knowing there wasn't any more, he put his spoon down and settled back into his chair.

The Lounge was full of the comfy red leather chairs. It was a long private room, hidden away in the Geography section of the Library. The wooden floor was littered with Persian rugs and at the far end a fire blazed in the hearth. Misty sat in the chair next to him, Martin and Randolph sat opposite, while in the centre were two trolleys. The first was laden with books, the second with exotic looking teas and thick chocolate biscuits. Along one wall stretched several black and white maps, the other walls were lined with books, older and more mysterious than any Kevin had seen before. Some had small faces emblazoned on their spines. They appeared to be sleeping, as if waiting for their allotted time when they would be pulled from the shelf to be read. And there were some Black books. Kevin could see them on the highest shelf behind Randolph. The sight of them sent a shiver down his spine.

'Misty J. Gilmore,' said Randolph, turning the first page in Misty's book. Misty sat on the edge of her seat, eager to know what was in a book that had her name on the front cover. Randolph began to read aloud. 'Your background ... hmm ... You're twelve years old.

You're bright and very athletic. You have two dogs, named Bubble and Squeak. You live in Upper Prendergast Road in the posh part of town and you go to Lady Oaks School. Correct?'

Kevin looked at Misty. She'd gone very white.

Randolph turned the page. 'You like to impress. Your arch-rival at school is Cynthia Slogitt and you hate it when she beats you at anything. You resent the fact that your mother and father make you work so hard, and you feel you have to get 'A' grades so they'll be pleased with you.' He turned another page. 'Ah! ... Here we are. Your dreams: you're saving your allowance so you can buy a horned toad like Jimmy's; you'd like to be an artist or a computer designer; you want to own your own house with a vegetable garden and you want to go to Africa and work ...'

'How do you know that?' interrupted Misty, jumping to her feet. She pointed angrily at the book. 'Who's been spying on me? It's not true! ... It's not! ... And even if it was, who could possibly know all that?' She made an angry rush for the book, but Martin stood and barred her way.

'Sit down, sit down!' said Randolph. 'I'm just reading what it says.'

'How does it know?' Misty pointed accusingly at the book.

'The books know everything,' soothed Martin.

'Please!' said Randolph gently. 'Sit down, so I can carry on ... Thank you.'

Kevin swallowed and wriggled his toes uncomfortably as Randolph picked up the second book.

'Kevin,' said Randolph, reading the cover. He opened the book. 'You're brave and honest and you've started a new school ... You have a dream, but only one. More than anything, you want to see your father again.' A huge lump welled up in Kevin's throat. The book knew. He wanted to cry.

Randolph closed the book and looked at Martin. 'What do you think?'

Martin nodded.

'I agree.' Randolph turned to the children. 'I'm pleased that you have those dreams, but ...' he held up both books and flicked through the pages. Most of them were blank ... 'there's room for plenty more.'

'More what?' asked Misty, 'I don't understand!'

'More dreams!' The gibbon put down the books, took off his glasses and placed them on the side table. He squeezed the top of his nose. 'Let me try to explain. A dream is something you want to happen in the future. When you dream, you're planning to change the future.'

> ## 'A dream is something you want to happen in the future.'

Randolph paused when he saw their confused faces. 'Let me put it another way ...' He pointed to the wall. 'Dreams are like a map. When you dream you're mapping out your future. But if you've no map, then you don't know where to go! That's why dreams are powerful - they map your future - they give you direction and hope.'

'Is that why people's books are in the Future section?' asked Misty.

'Exactly!' said Randolph. 'Dreams change the future!' He sighed and offered the plate of chocolate biscuits. 'But most children don't realise that - that's why their books are often blank'.

'It's Azmo!' interrupted Martin. 'It's his fault. I hate him!'

'Calm down, Martin, calm down!' Randolph used his tail to pull Martin back to his chair. 'Yes, Azmo steals dreams. That's why he's called the Dream Stealer.' He looked at Misty and smiled. 'I know the truth sometimes hurts and I'm sorry I upset you. I didn't mean to.'

'I'm sorry too!' Misty said sheepishly. 'But why are dreams so important?'

Randolph watched the children munching their biscuits, before answering. 'When you have a dream you should do everything you can to make it come true, because, by making it come true, it's *then* you change the future!'

'And that's why Azmo steals dreams!' added Martin. '*He* wants to control the future!'

'But not yours!' Randolph held up

> 'When you have a dream you should do everything you can to make it come true, because, by making it come true, it's *then* you change the future!'

their books. 'Because now you know you can control your own future!'

Kevin dropped his head. Dreaming sounded great for everyone else, but not for him. He was stuck in a school for unwanted children. What future did he have? His book would always be blank. Azmo, whoever he was, had stolen his dreams already. 'Is that why you brought us here?' he mumbled. 'To teach us about dreams?'

'No,' Randolph leaned back in his chair. 'I didn't bring you here. He did.'

'He?' asked Misty, puzzled.

Randolph looked at Kevin. 'He was the one who told me that someone special with orange hair would one day arrive through the box.'

Kevin lifted his head. 'Who said that?'

'The Panaginip Bayan.' Randolph chuckled at their confused faces. 'It's a strange name, I know, but the Panaginip Bayan designed all the worlds and put them into books and gave them to us to look after.'

'He sounds exciting,' said Misty. 'Can we meet him?' She looked at Kevin and frowned. 'Kevin, what is it? What's wrong?'

Kevin had noticed something peculiar. On the shelf, right behind Randolph's head, was a book - a Black book and it was moving. It was wriggling forwards, as if someone were pushing it from behind. The face on its spine was straining hard, desperate to be free. Before Kevin could reply, the book flew from the shelf and hit Randolph clear across the back of his head. It sent the gibbon somersaulting into a trolley that crashed to the floor, strewing its books everywhere. Martin jumped up and looked at the Black book sitting in the middle of the floor. Smoke was seeping from its pages.

BANG! The book pivoted violently open, making everyone jump. A large cloud of red smoke billowed out. Kevin dived behind his chair and peered around the arm. There was something in the smoke - he could just make out a shadow. It turned and floated past Randolph's unconscious body towards Misty. The shadow stopped and raised a knobbly claw. A siren began to scream.

'It's Azmo!' Martin shouted from somewhere in the smoke. 'Look out!'

'FLASH!' A blinding bolt of energy fizzed from the claw, momentarily bathing Misty in a white glow before she disappeared. Kevin stood up, shocked, but he had no time to think. The claw was pointing at him.

FLASH! FLASH! Two more lightning volts streaked across the room narrowly missing Kevin who dived sideways. The chair erupted into flames and the bookcase behind wobbled, causing several books to fall to the floor. He glanced round - the whole bookcase was toppling towards him. He gave a cry of horror and threw up his arms to protect himself, but as he did, he accidentally touched the open pages of a falling book and promptly vanished.

WHAM! WHAM! WHAM! WHAM! Ten thousand more books, including the whole A-Z of the unabridged *Encyclopaedia of Distant Universes and Beyond*, crashed onto Azmo, burying him completely.

The door burst open and a dozen gorillas and an army of monkeys charged into the smoke. Martin leapt to Randolph's side and helped him up. The gibbon rubbed his sore head and looked around in bewilderment. Monkeys were everywhere, extinguishing fires and lovingly rescuing precious books. Others were trying to recapture a mix of long-eared creatures that had escaped from another world. One monkey was stuffing a croaking monster back into its book; another duelled bravely with a nasty-looking medieval knight.

'Quickly!' Martin shouted to a couple of gorillas. 'Move the books!'

Minutes later Martin was reporting to Randolph. 'Azmo's gone ... so have the children.' He handed an open book to Randolph. 'This is all we've got. Kevin touched its pages and disappeared into it.'

'THE WORLD OF THE DEADLY DICE' read the title page.

Randolph groaned as he looked at the cover - it was a Black book.

Chapter 11

Hobnobs

Plob's gum ached. No, it hurt, *really* hurt! A dirty rag was tied around his jaw as he shuffled through the dark labyrinth of caves and passages. His hand clutched a candle and his thoughts wandered. Perhaps, if he were faithful for another hundred years, master would let him go? Perhaps he would be allowed his teeth and missing fingers back?

The candle revealed a left-hand fork in the passage, making Plob pause. He never liked going down this tunnel. This was where his master's Collection was kept. He could hear them screaming in their pits. They were hungry - always hungry. His master called them 'pets' and 'experiments'. Plob was afraid of them.

The bumbling dwarf unlocked a wooden door set back in the grey rock and pulled out a bucket of red worms. He wrinkled up his nose and entered the left-hand passage.

A few minutes later Plob re-emerged from the tunnel, exhausted. The creatures had indeed been ravenous. It had taken eleven buckets of eel slop, several handfuls of lizard gizzards and the whole bucket of red worms to satisfy them. Plob returned to the main cave just in time to see a door appear in mid air.

The door unzipped itself. Firstly across the top, then down to the ground and finally back across the floor. The door opened, the air shimmered and his master stepped through.

Azmo turned and meticulously rolled it up, storing it in his sleeve. The magic door was his preferred way of travelling.

'Plob, where are you?'

Azmo's jabbing, yellow eye analysed Plob for a moment, as if considering doing something particularly unpleasant. Instead, he rubbed his aching head and glided unsteadily over to his armchair. He pushed aside his *Book of Death* and clambered into the chair.

It wasn't everyday that a mountain of books fell on him. He spat out a last remnant of red smoke powder in disgust. The boy had escaped, disappeared into an adjoining world! He pushed aside his *Book of Death* and picked up a magazine, trying to compose his maddened thoughts into some kind of logic. But he had captured the girl. At least he could add her to his Collection, and one more child in it was one less child to worry about.

'Here mathter ... I hath your blanket ...' Plob barged clumsily back into the cave.

'Do you know why I need a blanket?' interrupted Azmo, picking up a magazine. 'It's to protect me from your hosepipe of a mouth, you oversized spitting cobra! Every time I come home it's like being dipped in a bath of mucus!'

'Thorry mathter!' Plob trembled.

'Stop it! Stop it! Stop it!' shrieked Azmo wiping his sleeve. 'This is my last clean robe! Go and do something useful and light the fire. I like it hot - very hot. And don't speak to it, you might put it out!'

Plob scuttled away to fetch some wood while his master scanned the latest edition of *Evil Weekly*. Azmo always looked forward to its delivery, though it was a trifle annoying that it always arrived late, but such was the price to pay for living under a volcano. Of course, there were advantages: no infernal door-to-door salesmen, instant hot water and his very own garbage incinerator - even if the paperboy was sometimes 'accidentally' incinerated! The way the paperboy's hair flared up and his eyes sizzled in their sockets was always most amusing - provided it happened *after* he'd made his delivery. Azmo scanned the headlines, tutting occasionally.

Plob returned, balancing a tall pile of dry timber, which he dropped noisily beside the fire's blackened cooking pots and utensils, upsetting a nesting family of black widow spiders.

Oh, and I'd like a cup of gnat tea and a chocolate Hobnob,'

demanded Azmo, not bothering to look up.

Plob hastily brushed the previous night's ashes from the hearth, creating a small dust cloud.

'What are you doing now? Suffocating me?' coughed Azmo, turning the page and glaring at Plob.

'There are no chocolate oneths left,' mumbled Plob. He gulped as Azmo slowly lowered his magazine.

'No chocolate ones?' asked Azmo suspiciously. 'You haven't been scoffing them on the side have you?'

'We've run out.'

Plob tried to ignore Azmo's eyes, which seemed to bore into his very soul.

'Run out? Run out? They obviously saw you, that's why - you frilled lizard! Ha! Ha! Ha!' Azmo laughed raucously at his own taunt. He was feeling better already. He had failed to terminate the boy but everything was still in hand. How he hated children. They had potential, much more potential than they realised. They could *dream* and they had their whole lives ahead of them to make those dreams come true, which is why they needed to be eliminated, or even better ... corrupted!

'Plain Hobnobs will have to do,' sighed Azmo, returning to the

> **How he hated children. They had potential, more potential than they realised. They could dream ...**

magazine. Hmmmm! Things weren't going so well in the other lands. The White Witch was having problems with the Lion again and the Ring Lord was struggling to keep the Halflings in order. But at least he, Azmo, was doing well. *His* master would be proud of him.

'OWWWWW!' Azmo was jerked into the present as a scolding pain seared his arm. His brew had arrived, albeit in the wrong place, spilt by his trembling servant.

'Plob! You ... you have as much grace as a chicken riding a firework! First you try and drown me, then suffocate me and now blister me! I've had enough!' Azmo pointed his claw.

BANG! There was a flash of blue smoke and Plob was reduced to a lump of green jelly.

Azmo sighed. Peace at last. He looked at the remains of his steaming drink and frowned.

Letting out an exasperated sigh, he pointed his claw at the smoking green blob.

BANG! Again there was a flash and once again Plob stood before him, wide-eyed and slightly charred.

'Hobnobs,' said Azmo. 'You forgot the Hobnobs.' Plob turned and obediently staggered to the pantry. 'And I still need something to dip them in. Preferably *in* the cup this time!'

Azmo leaned back in his chair, watching the flames dance in the grate. He smiled.

Hobnobs really would be his downfall.

Chapter 12

The Deadly Dice

As the bookcase tipped forwards, Kevin disappeared from the Library into the pages of the Black book. His feet landed on something hard. The floor tilted, causing him to topple sideward and a spray of seawater slapped him in the face. The floor moved again and a second spray sent him spluttering backwards.

'Save yourself!' A large bald man with a face like a trout was shouting at him. 'The boat can't take anymore. We're doomed!'

Kevin grabbed a wooden railing. His mind was working overtime. What was he doing aboard a boat?

'Rocks dead ahead! Rocks!' someone screamed.

Another wave drove in hard, washing Kevin's feet from under him. Freezing cold water dripped down his neck. Snow swirled around him. A pile of cannonballs crashed past and high above a set of grey sails bulged greedily forwards, tugging madly on the creaking rigging.

Suddenly there was an ominous scrape, followed by a fearful grinding. Kevin was flung into the air as the boat juddered to a halt, breaking its back on the rocks.

'AAAAAAAAAAAAAAAAAAAAAAAAAAAaaaaaaaa … a … a … huh?'

Kevin hung motionless, as if someone had pushed a pause button, yet his mind was spinning. Everything had happened so quickly. Moments before he'd been in the Library, now he was on board a sinking boat. Even more confusing was the world around him that, without explanation, had come to a sudden halt. There was no noise, no movement, no life. Nothing seemed real. The bald man was frozen still as he fell overboard. A wicked streak of lightning hung suspended in the grey sky. The sea was silent, each crest clearly defined, as if captured on an oil painting. Even more unnerving was the gaping hole beneath him. He could see right through the splintered deck to the sea far below, as if he were perched on the lip of a terrifying roller coaster, waiting for it to restart and hoping it never would.

A hollow cough made Kevin look up. Right in front of him hovered a dice. It was bigger than a football and had a face etched on its one spot.

'Oh dearie, dearie me!' said the dice, looking at the hole. It spoke in the rich, singsong accent of the Welsh valleys. 'What a terrible predicament you've got yourself into. But if you ask me, you've only got yourself to blame!'

A second dice popped out of thin air. It was a number five that spoke the best Queen's English. 'Don't listen to him. No one likes Number One, well, apart from Number Two!'

'And what's wrong wi' Number Two? Hoots mon!' The Welsh one on the first dice had rolled over and been replaced by a Scottish two. 'You English fives are always lookin' doon yer noses thinkin' you're a six. Well, I've got news for ye, ye ain't.'

'Certainly not. He's one dot short.' The five had rolled to a gruff-

talking Cockney six. 'You need to roll me. I can help you every
time. I'm well connected! I know all the right moves!'

'How could you know all ze right moves?' interrupted a French
whine. 'You're Eenglish!' Kevin looked back to the first dice who
had now become a grumpy French three. 'You have no style and
you smell of curry!'

The second dice flipped to a female Irish four. 'To be fair, don't be harsh now. I love Number Six. After all, together we make a perfect ten!'

'Excuse me!' said Kevin butting in. 'What's going on?'

'Oh dearie, dearie me!' sing-songed the Welsh one. 'It's time to explain the "rules"!' Kevin's mind whirled as he tried to keep up with the two dice as they changed back and forth. 'What do you mean? What rules?'

'The rules of our world, of course!' said Number Six. 'Honestly, am I surrounded by idiots or what?' This last statement was met by a load of grumbling from the other dice until it finally rolled to a second number six. 'Finally! Intelligent conversation,' said the first six.

'Now,' said the sixes in unison, hovering in front of Kevin, 'the rules! Basically, you've stepped into *our* world! And in our world, you can do what you want, except in tense moments like this. It's then that we appear and roll for you, and, depending on the roll, you might get out of the mess you're in, or you might not. So, if you roll a pair of super sixes, you'll be stocking-and-tights alright! Double one and you're gone, plop down the swanny! Understand?' Kevin eyed the sea below. 'So, what you're saying is that I'm allowed to do what I want, but if I get in trouble, then *you* decide what happens?'

'In not so many words, yes!'

'That's a bit unfair!'

'Well, that's the way it rolls,' said the sixes. 'It's *our* book! And looking at your situation now, you definitely need to roll a five or above. But don't worry ... you can trust us!'

'Hang on ...' Before Kevin could say anymore, the two dice whirled in the air. Round and round they spun, getting ready to seal Kevin's fate.

PLOP! The first dice landed on the deck below.

'Oh dearie, dearie me! Looks like you could be in trouble, boyo!' shouted up a Welsh one. Kevin gulped, helpless as he watched the second dice land.

PLOP! He was OK! It was a four! He'd rolled a total of five!

'Oh, don't you be fretting, Irish eyes are smiling! Four and one makes five! You're fine.'

'No he's not!' hooted Scottish Two, pushing Irish Four out the way. 'He's doomed, he's only rolled a total of three!'

'Hang on, that's cheatingggggggggggggg!' Kevin's panicked cry was lost as everything began to move again and he plummeted through the hole into the water below.

KERPLOSH! Black water swirled over his head, pulling him straight through the broken hull and into the stormy sea. He surfaced and gasped for air, trying to keep his mouth above the icy water. He could see the boat close by. As he tried to swim towards it, a spray of salty seawater lashed against his face. He wiped his eyes, but as he did a thundering wave swept over him. After what seemed an age, his head broke the surface, but almost immediately another wave pulled him under.

The sea was toying with him, throwing him recklessly back and forth. The cold was affecting him. His strength was going. The storm was too fierce. He wasn't going to make it.

Chapter 13

A Bit of a Shock

The undercurrent pulled him towards the rocks, but instead of battering him against the black boulders, it swept him down a thin channel into a secluded bay. Kevin flapped weakly towards the shore. Wading out of the water, he collapsed, exhausted, on the pebbles. His legs felt like lead, his back ached and his teeth chattered.

Towering cliffs surrounded him on every side. Gulls huddled on outcroppings, their screeching barely audible above the howling wind. Stumbling forwards, he forced himself towards a crevice in the cliff. Sharp rocks tugged at his clothes as he squeezed through a narrow opening and collapsed on a patch of dry sand.

Why had the dice let him fall into the sea? He'd almost died. Had it been an accident or was that what the dice had wanted? He felt cold and confused. It wasn't fair - but neither was how he'd been treated at school or how he'd been picked on. Nor was it fair how the box had changed the way he looked. Nothing was fair!

Slowly his breathing calmed and he looked around - he was in a small cave. Feeling sorry for himself wouldn't do him any good. He'd keep going - that's what his father would have wanted. Scrambling up, he looked around for something to burn, though he didn't know how he would light a fire without matches. After collecting a pile of dry seaweed and old fishing netting which had been washed into the cave from past storms, he began groping in the darkness at the back of the cave, hoping to find a stick that he could rub to start a fire. Instead his hand brushed against something soft. Grabbing hold, he tugged. It was heavy and would hardly budge, but as he kept pulling, it slowly gave way into the light.

It was a rucksack - but it was attached to something that made his heart jump - a human skeleton. The eye-sockets stared eerily. There was a dull crack as the skull snapped off, bounced twice on a boulder and rolled in a semi-circle across the sandy floor, eventually coming to a stop by the cave entrance. Kevin took a couple of deep breaths and slowly undid the rucksack's rusty buckles, trying to ignore the watching skull. He tipped the contents onto the ground: several tins of food, a compass, a penknife, a coil of thin rope, some spare clothes and best of all, a box of matches. He was saved - he just hoped the matches weren't damp! As he stooped to pick up the box, he noticed something strange ... something that made his heart start to race ... the skeleton only had *one* foot.

The left foot was missing! A cold clammy rush swept over him as Lawrence Pudding-Pig's story came to mind. Was this the missing boy from Greystones ... or was it just coincidence? He shuddered and concentrated on trying to light a match. To his delight the first match flared up straightaway.

Kevin was soon warming himself by a small fire, watching the

seaweed crackle, pleased at how well his new fur-lined jacket and leather trousers fitted him. The headless skeleton was propped up opposite and the skull was outside. Crossing his legs, he opened his second tin of peaches and stabbed a slice of tinned ham with the penknife. A shrill beep interrupted his meal and made him look at his watch. Words were scrolling across the screen - it was a text message.

< IT ME MISTY > said the words. Kevin gave a shout. Misty was alive!
< DON'T KNOW IF YOU GET THIS. DARK N SMELLY HERE. SCARED. HELP! >

Kevin banged the sand in frustration. How could he? He was as lost and stuck as she was - he couldn't even text a reply. When no other text came, he slipped his shoes on and disappeared into the back of the cave to gather another armful of driftwood.

Ten minutes later he was huddled by the flames, glad of their warmth. Thoughts of the Library, Martin and Misty rushed through his mind. He thought of Greystones and Azmo and the terrifying storm. It had been a long day, but he'd survived. Before long his thoughts were drifting and he was asleep.

Chapter 14

A Little Game

Kevin jumped. Something had prodded his side. He sat up, alarmed. The fire had gone and it was pitch black and cold.

He could hear something shuffling across the cave floor.

'Who's there?' His heart was thumping. Something was in the cave.

Another prod.

Kevin scrambled backwards, frightened. A silhouette waddled across the cave entrance. 'Who is it?'

More shuffling followed by a loud 'click'. Eerie blue light flooded the cave making Kevin blink. Tall, mean-looking penguins, each about Kevin's size and all armed with three-pronged tridents, surrounded him.

He was scared and tried to move away, but the penguins thrust their tridents towards him, forcing him towards a hidden doorway at the back of the cave, from where the blue light was coming. He ducked through the doorway into a secret tunnel, which was tall enough for him to stand in. Another prod forced him forwards. The penguins pattered behind. Walls, rough and hewn from stone,

banked to the left and right
before descending deeper
under the cliff.

Before long, Kevin heard
the faint sound of rushing
water, which grew steadily
louder. He assumed it was
the sea and shivered,
remembering the storm.
The penguins came to a
halt. A waterfall, spanning
the entire width of the

tunnel, blocked their path. Kevin gazed into the falling waters,
awed by the shimmering colours and thundering noise. The
mesmerising spell was broken only when the lead penguin pushed
its trident into the water, causing a long hole to appear. The
penguin gestured with his beak for Kevin to go through. He
ducked under the drips and the waterfall closed behind him.

He was in a cubicle and in the floor was a hole, the type you would
expect to see at the top of a water flume ride, and a mat lay beside
it. The hole was lit with the same blue light and, as far as he could
see, appeared to slope gently downwards. It was the only way out,
so Kevin climbed onto the mat, steadied himself and bravely
pushed off.

The mat slipped quietly into the tunnel before picking up speed.

Kevin leaned back and gripped tightly, wondering if he'd made the right decision. The tunnel tipped to the left and to the left again. It slowed before dropping dramatically. Kevin gritted his teeth as he flew down the icy tunnel. A white light rushed to meet him. The tunnel gave a flip, and he was spun round and round across a smooth floor, before sliding to a stop between the front legs of a huge animal.

The animal lowered its shaggy head and gave a long deliberate sniff. Kevin didn't dare move. It was a polar bear, bigger than a car and smelling of hot fish. Kevin shuddered and closed his eyes as the bear licked its lips.

'I'm hungry,' said the bear. 'You don't have any fish on you, by any chance?'

Kevin opened his eyes. The bear could talk!

'Do you?'

Kevin shook his head.

'Oh!' said the bear in its slow, dopey voice. 'How about chocolate, then? I do like chocolate.'

Kevin nodded warily.

'So, you have some then?'

'No.'

'Oh!' said the bear, looking disappointed.

It scratched its head with a big paw, thinking hard. 'Are you sure you don't have any chocolate?'

'Yes, I'm sure.'

'Oh!' said the bear sitting on its back haunches. 'I was just checking.' Kevin watched the bear over the bottom of his nose, still not daring to move.

'My foot's itchy!' said the bear. It looked at Kevin, as if expecting a reply.

'I, err, you'd better scratch it then!' said Kevin politely.

'Oh yeah!' said the bear, raising a pair of hairy eyebrows. 'I hadn't thought of that.' The bear scratched its leg. It stopped and stared at Kevin, 'Is your hair orange?'

'Yes,' said Kevin.

'Good,' said the bear. 'I'm colour-blind, but now I know you're him, I can take you in. You seem too nice, though ... Are you sure you don't have any chocolate?'

'Quite sure,' nodded Kevin, slowly sitting up. They were in a room, about the size of a house and not unlike the inside of a large igloo. The walls were white and curved, and at the far end was what looked like a glass door.

'Follow me,' said the bear. 'He'll be so pleased to see you ... He told me that if the penguins found you, you'd be coming down the chute and I was to take you in ... You really do seem too nice. Never mind, this way ... '

'Too nice for what?' Kevin followed the bear reluctantly. The door, which was made of a single slab of ice, led into a huge cavern covered in icicles, which rose from the floor and fell from the ceiling. Kevin's chin dropped as he gazed around at the glistening ice sculptures.

More spectacular still, was the giant who was staring at him. He appeared to be a king for he wore a crown and was seated on a throne inlaid with pearls and shells.

'*Veish fam oosh*,' the King boomed in a strange watery-sounding voice. He beckoned Kevin closer. The King had a monstrous white beard and blue eyes that blazed like a merciless blizzard. Behind the throne stood a row of magnificently carved marble seahorses. Their heads were held high and proud, as if they were riding into battle. To either side of the throne were a number of strange creatures: a mermaid with light skin and long eyelashes who casually swished her tail; a couple of sea lions and a sprawling walrus who was being used as a sort of sofa bed by two penguins. The walrus's stained tusks gave him an air of age and wisdom. All the creatures seemed unusually large. The bear sat down next to the King. Kevin felt rather intimidated, as if he were in a staff room with all the teachers looking at him.

'Yes!' the King spoke so that Kevin could understand. He gave a crooked smile, as if he knew something Kevin didn't. 'You will be perfect! Come closer ... that's it. Oh, you look different to most human children. You look all rubbery, but never mind, I'm sure you'll put up a good fight.'

'A fight?' said Kevin, feeling uneasy.

'The dice told me you have orange hair,' continued the King. 'They said they'd lost you in the sea and that if I found you, I should let

you play the game. My penguins have been looking all night. I'm so pleased. I can hardly wait. Would you like to start straight away, or would you like to eat first? There's clam soup or, if you prefer, there's herring '

'What game?' Kevin shuffled his feet.

'*Apporzs'eym eyn oijnder*!' said the King, turning to the animals, who laughed - all except the bear.

'Just a little game,' smiled the King. 'We'll ... I mean, *you'll* love it!'

Suddenly, a sheet of ice rose from the floor, separating Kevin from the King. The wall behind Kevin dropped, revealing a glorious panorama: a sweeping green lake bordered on all sides by sheer cliffs. Centre stage, in the middle of the lake, stood a tower made of blue stone. Between Kevin and the tower stretched a line of stepping-stones.

'All you have to do is get to the tower!' The King's laugh echoed across the glassy water. 'Enjoy the game!'

Kevin was puzzled. What game? He looked around suspiciously. Everything looked so peaceful.

The silence was broken by a loud crunching noise as the ice wall behind him started to move, forcing him forwards onto the first stepping-stone. He gave a little cry as the stone dipped slightly, nearly making him loose his balance.

He composed himself and looked around. Was the game not to fall off the stones? He stepped onto the second stone. Nothing. He hopped to the third and then the fourth. The stone tipped, making him crouch to keep balance. A scaly head appeared by his toes and an eye looked at Kevin briefly, before disappearing beneath the surface. He wasn't standing on a stone, but the back of a giant green turtle!

A wave rose from the lake on his right, towering over him. Kevin wobbled as he looked into the hovering wall of water. He could see hundreds of fish with sharp teeth. At the same moment, a shadow passed silently beneath him, while to his left a tail sent warning ripples across the watery surface. A cheer rang out from the hidden throne room as Kevin grasped the awful truth: he was the centre of a game of certain death, with as much hope as a blindfolded chick in a bowl of starving piranha.

Chapter 15

Never Trust Dice

As Kevin hopped from the back of one turtle shell to the next, he tried desperately not to look into the water. Concentrating hard, he hopped from shell to shell. He stopped and watched a shadow flit across the water. It looked purposeful in its movement and Kevin had a feeling of dread as he watched it.

A black fin broke the surface. With a cry of terror Kevin turned and dashed desperately for the tower. He slid across the shells, trying hard to ignore the shouts of amusement that echoed from the

hidden throne room. Suddenly, his foot slipped. He leapt towards the next shell but fell short, splashing into the water, only able to grab hold with his arms. He scrabbled at the shell, conscious of his legs that dangled helplessly in the water. Out the corner of his eye he saw the fin turn and then disappear beneath the surface. He kicked and clawed at the shell desperately, trying to force his way back onto the shell, but his hands slipped on the wet surface. The fin was coming straight for him. With a final burst of energy he pulled himself onto the shell just as the shadow passed beneath.

He gasped for breath and watched the fin surface and circle in the distance. Like an underwater torpedo, it was picking up speed and cutting towards him. Kevin turned to the tower. Could he reach the door in time? There were nine shells to go, then eight and then seven and then six. He could sense the shark behind him - only yards away - but so was the door ... could he get there?

The shark loomed out of the water, its eyes empty, unfeeling and

with one purpose in mind. Chiselled teeth gleamed as it opened its mouth wide. He wasn't going to make it!

Kevin opened his mouth to scream, but no sound came. Once again, as if someone had pushed 'Pause', everything froze.

'Waheeeeeeeeeeeey!' The cheerful Irish dice popped out of the terrifying, but now stationary, shark jaws. 'Aren't you glad to see us right now?'

'Smelly as rotting rot in there!' said the well-spoken English five, joining Irish Four from inside the shark. 'Wouldn't go in there if I were you, old boy!' he said, addressing Kevin who was suspended in mid-hop.

'I'll do my best!' croaked Kevin, eyeing the jagged jaws. His heart was thumping and he was doing his best not to look into the shark's black eyes.

'Right! Well, that's settled then,' said Number Five. 'You don't get eaten and we dice will have tea and cakes on top of the cliff. Splendid! Anyone got a cricket bat?'

'Aren't ye forgettin' somethin', ye haggis-brained excuse fer a dice?' interrupted Scottish Two, bashing into the first dice. 'The tower door's locked! He doesn't stand a chance. He's doomed, doomed, DOOMED!'

'Locked?' said Kevin hopelessly. 'Locked?'

'That's right!' said Cockney Six. 'But I think we could tweak a few rules. If you can roll a twelve we could get you out of here. Sort of a favour, like.'

'Twelve?' said Kevin. 'Like I'm really going to roll a twelve!'

'Yer not! Yer DOOMED!' laughed Scottish Two. 'You'll soon be in that shark's big teethie ... Not that we're *loaded dice*!'

'What?' said Kevin crossly. 'Loaded? You mean you're cheating?'

'Cheating? Us? No! ... well ... maybe just a wee bit!' Number Two flipped to a five, who stammered before twisting into another Welsh one, who stared at the other one, who in turn was whistling and doing his best to look anywhere but at Kevin. The ones flipped to twos who shuffled to fours who flipped, finally, to a pair of French threes.

> ## 'Anyone with 'alf a brain knows not to trust dice.'

'THRUPPPPPPPP! Who cares, anyway, you snotty leettle kid? Anyone with 'alf a brain knows not to trust dice. Anyway, it eez our world and we can do what we want! You were lucky last time, but not zis time. So, you better say *au revoir*, because it eez time to roll!' The French threes jumped up in a pathetic hop, landing with a little plop, onto the shark's tongue. 'Double three! Oh, *quelle dommage*! Bad luck!'

'Hey!' said Kevin. 'That isn't fair! You didn't roll properly! You went up in the air and landed exactly where you started.'

'Exactly? ... No, we did not.'

'You cheated!'

'No, we did not!'

'Yes, you did, you cheats!'

'No, we started off over zere and now we're over 'ere, in ze shark's mouth - where, we remind you, eez where you will be very soon. No one beats ze dice - we always win! And, anyway, double three eez so so. It eez good and bad ...'

'What do you mean?' Kevin said dubiously.

'Ze bad news eez, you eez about to become fish food ... zat's after he's digested you, of course! Ze good news eez ... er ... zat ze action eez about to start.'

'No, wait!' said Kevin.

'Lights, camera, action ...' directed the French dice. 'Let's *roll* it ... Hoh, hoh, hoh ... Get it?'

The action restarted and the shark surged towards Kevin.

Chapter 16

The Pit of Despair

Of course, you're probably wondering what had happened to Misty. One moment she was in the Library, the next, in a flash, she had hurtled through a twisting tunnel of light and been dumped in an underground pit.

She'd been there for hours, listening to the wailing noises that floated through the surrounding caves. She'd tried to climb the walls, but each time had slipped back. Finally she slumped in the corner. A constant drip splashed on the muddy floor and with each drip Misty's head hung lower.

All alone!

The green slimy walls gurgled, as if sensing her despairing thoughts.

No one knew she was there.

Misty was so engrossed that she failed to notice the slime. It crept towards her with a sigh of delight, sticking to her like gooey fingers of caramel. The more she despaired the more it stuck.

The thoughts were overwhelming. There was something so evil and draining about the whole place that hope seemed like a far-off dream.

'Coooooweeeee!'

A high-pitched voice with a distinct Yorkshire flavour pierced through the gloom like a shaft of brilliant sunlight. 'Ee by gum, luv! Thou's in a right mess!'

Misty opened her eyes to see who was speaking. She couldn't see anyone but, to her horror, she saw the slime. She struggled, panic-stricken, but she was trapped. Worse still, the green tentacles began to crawl towards her mouth.

'Stuck tighter than ferret down a pair o' occupied jeans, eh?' The high-pitched squeak was coming from somewhere on the floor. 'Before tha know it, tha'll be covered all o'er in that stuff, snugger than jam roly-poly in me Aunty Mabel's lumpy custard!' Misty's eyes widened. Whoever was speaking didn't seem to care a bit. Couldn't they see the mess she was in? How dare they be so flippant!

'Oose toad in t' hole then, eh?'

'I'm not a toad! I'm a girl and my name's Misty!'

'Misty, eh? I'm Andy, pronounced like its spelt, A-N-D-Y, you know, with 'E' ... just like your name! Kateee, Andeee. Oooooo! In't that grand! Oh, tha could knock me o'er wi' a feather!' A bug-like creature hopped from the shadows. It landed on the slime, inches from Misty's nose. 'So what's tha done to upset 'im?' Andy was a small, green, transparent, jelly-looking bug, with two intensely blue eyes that blinked through extraordinarily long eyelashes. He was wearing nothing but a Yorkshire flat cap and a well-groomed moustache. 'Slime-bug!' said Andy, sensing Misty's thoughts. 'Slime-bug Andy at tha service! Ain't nowt I don't know 'bout slime!' The long eyelashes blinked repeatedly. 'Ee lass, tha's lucky

I came along otherwise tha'd be like rest. All trapped in these underground pits like currants in Eccles cake.'

'But who are you?' asked Misty.

'Dun't tha listen? Andy, t' slime-bug!' said the bug opening his eyes even wider.

'Serial number 00000001. I'm t'only one of me. Quite unique we are - well, I am. Actually, so are thee. We all are, aren't we? Aye! ... 'cept sheep! Ten-to-dozen in Yorkshire they are, not that I've been there lately ... or ever, actually. No! Sorry, I'm rambling ... not walking kind o'er moors ... aye, that's a right walk that is o'er moors, not that I've been there either. Eh, sorry, am I rambling? Not like walking ... oops, sorry, I've been here before, 'aven't I?'

Misty smiled. The rabbiting chatter of this strange creature was most amusing, especially in his high-pitched voice. Although

Andy didn't seem to be saying anything very helpful, his words were strangely comforting. Perhaps this wasn't the end after all.

'Slime!' squeaked Andy, excitedly remembering what he'd wanted to say in the first place and then immediately forgetting again. 'It's ... it's green ... like me! 'Cept tha can see right through me, like lovely stained-glass winder in York Cathedral ... not that I've ever bin to York, nor even t' cathedral for that matter and I don't right know what stained glass is, 'cept it's glass and it's stained ... like tea! Tea stains ...eee ...I could die for a cuppa! Well, not really die, 'cause then I'd be dead and I couldn't drink tea ... not that I've ever drunk tea, but I'm sure it'ud be nicer than slime. *Slime*! That's where I was ... me name's Andy, with an 'e' ... or 'ave I said that?'

'Yes!' said Misty, beginning to laugh. 'You have!'

'Eh? What's s' funny? I 'aven't turned pink, have I? I 'ate it when that 'appens! I feel like right blob of raspberry jam, right embarrassing! Mind you, it's only 'appened once. I swallowed one of them sweeties that one of them kids dropped ...'

'What kids?' interrupted Misty excitedly. 'Are there others here?'

''undreds and thousands. No, 'undreds. No, fifty or a bit more. Maybe ten. One or two even. Seven. I don't know! You? Look, I'm a slime-bug. I just live 'ere, tha sees, like slither 'ere, slither there, like a ... like a slitherin' thing in slime, oh aye! *Slime*! That's what I was on about! We've got to get thee out t' slime!'

Misty had completely forgotten about the slime. When she looked down she was surprised to see it had recoiled to below her knees.

'How did that happen?' she asked, sitting up and catapulting Andy onto the floor.

'Don't worry!' he chirped, before she could apologize. He picked

> **'Slime's only got power tha gives it - it feeds off tha negative thoughts.'**

himself up and adjusted his cap with a fold of slime. "Cause tha didn't think 'bout it! Slime's only got power tha gives it - it feeds off tha negative thoughts. Look! Tha's free! Tha see, tha stopped thinking 'bout slime! Now tha ought to be thinking 'bout 'ow to get out before Dream Stealer gets back. These are 'is dungeons. I don't live 'ere. I work for Panaginip Bayan. Kind of like a spy, not that I've ever met spy ... I wouldn't even know spy if I saw one 'cause he'd be in disguise and so I wouldn't recognize 'im, would I? 'Cept me ... Aye! I'm not stupid! I'd recognize me if I was in disguise! Ee! By gum, I'm not stupid! Hold on, I just said that ... I'll tell tha secret though, just between two o' us ...'

For a second (and most unlike him) Andy stopped speaking and peeked over the space where his shoulder would have been if he'd had one - which he didn't being a slime-bug. Quickly he removed his moustache, then replaced it again. 'Disguise!' whispered Andy. 'I'm in disguise ... I've been put here by Panaginip Bayan t' spy ... just in case ...'

'Just in case, what?' said Misty. But Andy had disappeared. A shadow loomed over the place where he'd been standing. Something had scared him away. Slowly Misty looked up. A balding dwarf, with missing teeth, was staring down at her.

Chapter 17

The Mouse

A few minutes before Plob had been feeding his masters 'pets'. He had shivered as the beast in the pit glared at him with eleven of its eyes. The twelfth eye inspected the eel slop that had been rudely dumped at its tail. Plob had hastily edged back from the edge of the pit. How he hated feeding time. His master's 'pets' were always hungry. Plob had carried the empty buckets back through the caves, stopping only to avoid a tentacle that writhed hungrily out of one of the pits. An unpleasant decaying smell filled the air. Plob sidestepped the tentacle and continued down a tunnel.

Each 'pet' lived in its own pit and constantly needed checking to ensure the 'process' was working. When they first arrived they looked so normal, but in the end they looked ... Plob winced and tried not to think of the monsters that lived in the pits: pits of greed, unforgiveness, hatred, jealousy and despair. Each pit transformed its captive into the monster that had always been hidden deep within them. Plob paused at a doorway carved in the side of the tunnel. 'PIT 19' was scrawled in chalk on the wall and he remembered that a new 'pet' had been put in there only today.

He had hurried past and continued down the tunnel, not wanting to disturb the creature. It might shoot out a venom-coated elastic tongue or do something equally nasty - you never could tell with the new ones.

But he'd stopped all of a sudden. A nagging feeling told him he ought to check on the creature's progress. Why, he didn't know. Perhaps it was the fear of being in trouble if anything was wrong. Putting down his buckets, he crept back down the tunnel. He tiptoed into the cave, not wanting to be heard - that only made them angrier. Four lanterns, equally spaced around the circular walls, illuminated a hole, three metres wide, in the middle of the floor. Plob had listened to the creature chattering to itself. Now he dropped to his knees and shuffled closer. Clasping the edge, he slowly pulled himself forward and peered into the pit.

How strange. The creature was still normal. He had expected the slime to have covered it by now. Plob hurriedly backed away as the creature looked up.

'Hello!' It was speaking to him! Probably lulling him into a false sense of security. 'Hello!' said the creature again, cheerfully. 'I'm Misty! Can you help? I'm stuck. I mean you can see that yourself, and ... well, I'd like to escape.'

Escape? A rush of emotions swept over Plob. He blinked awkwardly, trying not to let his feelings show. Escape!

'Did I say something wrong?' The creature had noticed, but hold on ... why was the creature asking how he was? No one had ever asked him that before. Perhaps it was a trap! Master was testing his loyalty.

'Oh, you poor thing!' cried Misty. 'You've only got two fingers!' There was something pathetic and sad about Plob's face that made

Misty feel sorry for him. 'How did that happen?'

Plob hurriedly pulled his hand out of sight. He couldn't remember which finger had been used for what experiment but before he knew it he'd begun to explain.

> 'This one was different. It was interested in someone other than itself.'

'Mathher does spells with ...' He stopped, amazed. He'd never spoken to a creature before. Normally they just drooled and roared ... but this one didn't. This one was different. It was interested in someone other than itself. Even in its miserable circumstances it was concerned about *him*. A surge of warm fuzziness swept through Plob: a sense of worth and acceptance that brought a tear to his eye. Not for a long time had he experienced such a wonderful feeling.

'I'm Misty!' said the creature again. 'Who are you?'

'Plob!'

Oh you poor, *poor* thing!' said the Misty creature. 'You've hardly got any teeth! What happened to them?'

'Mathter ... he ... he ... he uses them!' said Plob, hurriedly wiping the tear from his eye. He could listen to that kind voice all day. No one had shown any interest in him for such a long time.

Misty was shocked. 'Uses your teeth? Uses them!' She shuddered.

How could anyone do something like that? Another thought entered her mind, a frightening one. Perhaps the person who'd taken Plob's teeth would want to take hers! She looked into Plob's sad eyes. 'You have to help me escape ... *please*?'

Plob's eyes widened.

Escape! That word taunted him, as if he were a mouse confronted by cheese on a mousetrap. And that's all he was ... a mouse! A mouse who lived underground and obeyed every beck and call of his evil master; a mouse who used to dream of escape, but who never would. The Dream Stealer had stolen his dream a long time ago.

Plob slowly and shamefully withdrew into the darkness, distancing himself from the lovely but misguided creature. It would mutate soon. He would leave it alone until the slime changed it into yet another ghastly monster, one who was as uncaring as the rest, one who wouldn't cause such dangerous feelings to emerge.

'No,' Plob thought, 'I will never escape. I'm a mouse: a fingerless, toothless, useless mouse.'

Chapter 18
Plob's Story

Plob slumped into a shadowy corner of the tunnel. It hadn't always been like this. He closed his eyes and remembered ...

Uncle Poggy was one of a rare breed of dwarfs who lived in the happy hill-lands of Gweeshmoor-on-the-Flat. Of course, it wasn't *always* a happy place. There'd been the occasional encounter with an ogre or a skirmish with a prowling goblin, yet despite these irregular scuffles, Gweeshmoor-on-the-Flat had, for the most part, been a peaceful place to live. And no dwarf had been happier than Plob's Uncle Poggy. As village cobbler, he'd enjoyed mending the other dwarfs' shoes and then, at the end of each day, sitting on the porch of his house with his best friend Pod. Each would suck on their liquorish sherbet twist and see whose tongue would turn blue first, with the winner being allowed to jump up and down and do the winner's 'blue-tongue-gecko-king' dance before putting a jar of millipedes down the loser's trousers.

All that had changed one night.

There was a violent thunderstorm. The pounding of the rain was so fierce that even the village fish were cowering under the lily pads. Plob could remember looking out of his Uncle Poggy's bedroom window, marvelling at the great sheets of falling water as they emptied themselves down on the sleeping village. Flashes of lightning sent long shadows flitting across the trees. And then, through the night, silhouetted against forked-lightning flashes, came a hoard of silent figures: some on horseback, some hunched, others on four legs. All had fearsome weapons: double-handed broadswords, wicked hooked pikes and bone-crushing war hammers. This was the Army of Fear, an ugly snarling tidal wave of destruction that was marching to war.

Little Plob watched wide-eyed as a monstrous shape separated itself from the trudging hoard and crossed toward their cottage. Plob gulped as the garden gate was ripped effortlessly from its hinges and tossed through the air. There was a warning rumble in the heavens above. A jagged grin of lightening streaked above the unfortunate cottage.

There followed three short raps upon the front door. Plob turned in his window seat and gazed at the bedroom door. He heard his uncle stir from his armchair. There was another knock and a disgruntled mutter before a sudden CRASH and a cry of alarm. Then there was a shriek, a scream, some noisy crunching and then silence.

Ominous silence.

And then a sick, gut-wrenching feeling as Plob heard a resounding THUD, the type of noise that a heavy boot makes on a wooden staircase.

THUD!

The ogre sniffed the air. He could smell dwarf. Another dwarf. He wiped his blubbery lips. One dwarf was never enough.

THUD!

The ogre's hand clasped the banister, which snapped beneath its weight.

THUD!

He ducked under the low landing ceiling and rammed his heavy boot into the first of the two wooden doors. CRASH! Nothing but a teeny pan of water and a dangling metal chain! But how convenient - some light refreshment before the main course. The ogre's purple tongue reached out and sucked up the bowl's contents. It tasted rather tangy, but was refreshing nevertheless. The ogre turned to leave, only to notice the magical appearance of a new clearer bowlful of water - a bowlful of water that was again thirstily consumed, and once again replaced by yet another pan of water. The ogre scratched its small head.

CRASH! The second door splintered into pieces. The ogre's hairy eyebrows knitted themselves together in puzzlement. Its bloodshot eyes surveyed the empty bedroom. He could smell dwarf, yet there was none in sight. All he could see was a chest of drawers, an oak stool and a bed with a large lump under the covers. He would never understand dwarfs. How on earth could they sleep with such lumpy mattresses?

The ogre roared in frustration. The bed was sent hurtling over his shoulder; the stool was ripped apart and pinned deep into the plasterwork; the drawers were randomly dispersed into next-

door's cabbage patch. And then, not content with one room's worth of destruction, the ogre set about reducing the whole cottage to a pile of sticks before leaving in disgust. The annoying thing was he could *still* smell dwarf!

The lump that had been hiding beneath the blankets had, of course, been Plob, who, as the bed was smashed against the far corner of the room, had dropped into the ogre's backpack and been carried, much to the frustration of the keen-smelling giant, to the battlefield.

During the battle, an arrow had felled the ogre, allowing Plob to escape. He had run, ducking and diving through the battle's bloody aftermath, until, in the fading twilight, he had accidentally crashed into a darkly-robed figure.

Plob sighed. Things could have been worse. As punishment, Azmo had made him his slave. And for the next three hundred and seventy-five years Plob had watched his master grow smaller and weaker in physical form, but stronger and darker in magical powers.

A roar shocked Plob back to the present. He opened his eyes and remembered where he was. Struggling to his feet, he set off down the tunnel with his buckets. His heart was heavy. How he missed home. But that Misty creature had been nice to him. She reminded him of his Uncle Poggy, always thinking of others first.

A spark of hope began to grow in Plob, a spark that didn't want to be a mouse anymore, a spark that caused his feet to break into a run. He was going to attempt something brave, something foolish and something desperately dangerous.

Chapter 19
Annie Brig

Now it is here, just as the shark was lunging for Kevin, just as Misty was stuck in the Pit of Despair and just as Plob was deciding to do something desperately dangerous, that I must interrupt the whole story and introduce someone new to you. Her name was Annie Brig. She was a large girl and there's certainly nothing wrong with being large. The problem was that she was greedy and selfish - very greedy and selfish. She had arrived in one of Azmo's pits a few months before, in a most unfortunate manner. (This chapter is all about *how* she got there. I feel that it is important you know this, but it is also a bit scary, so please don't read it if you don't want to).

Annie Brig was large, *very* large - and it was completely her fault. Her mother called her 'my precious pudding', her doctor called her 'unusually proportioned' and her friends called her 'big fat porker!' Of course, they weren't real friends. Annie didn't have time for them. Why should she bother with friends when she had the fastest joystick this side of Tokyo!

To say that Annie Brig was mad about computer games would be the understatement of the millennium. It would be like saying that Albert Einstein was 'quite a clever bloke' or that breathing was a 'rather important thing to do'. Basically, Annie Brig was besotted. Way gone! She was the ultimate computer nerd - a gaming freak whose all-consuming desire was to get to the next level.

Every day, when Annie Brig finally managed to wobble out of her bed, she'd eat several bars of chocolate before turning on her laptop, and every day she would get so engrossed in her game that she'd be late for school. Her parents didn't care and her teachers had given up. She'd play on her laptop on the way to school, in playtime, on the way home again, and even on the toilet! Her aunty (who was rather blunt) said it was because she was too fat to do anything else. The doctor said she was addicted and that it was just a passing phase. *That* was three years ago.

The night it happened, it was seven o'clock. Annie was still only on level five of her new game. Her podgy fingers alternated between her sixth packet of crisps and her sweaty joystick as she feverishly fought ninja sheep.

'Bye, Annie!' her mother's shrill voice sounded from the hallway below. 'We're going out to dinner. See you later, my precious pudding!'

Annie ignored her mother as usual. The ninja sheep had joined forces with killer rams. Her joystick was a blur as she exterminated this new threat.

The front door closed with a dull click. A contented smile flickered across Annie's bloated cheeks. Now she was alone she could play her game in peace. This was a tricky level; she frowned and concentrated hard.

Zip! Zip! BLAM! BLAM! BLAM!

There was a knock on the front door.

'My parents must have forgotten something,' thought Annie, still concentrating on her game. 'I can't believe they're too lazy to use their own key!' Engrossed in her game, she forgot about the intrusion until a few minutes later when there came a second knock.

'I'm too busy!' thought Annie, 'and anyway, this is the good bit.' Now she was under pressure. More and more sheep were pouring over the hills. She really had to concentrate. ZAP! ZAP! ZAP! It was going to be close. Her fingers were working at a speed that seemed disproportionate to the rest of her out-of-shape-body. Finally, the last sheep was terminated! With a trumpet fanfare and a despairing bleat she knew she was victorious!

In celebration she reached for her crisps.

Hold on.

Had she heard something? She paused. Nothing. She must have imagined it. Her mouth closed around a wodge of crisps.

What was that?

She paused again with her mouth full. Something was making her uneasy. But surely it had only been her parents at the door and, anyway, all the doors and windows were locked. Pure imagination, that's all it was. She relaxed and started to crunch her crisps.

Creak.

She froze.

She was more than uneasy now. Something was wrong. Was someone playing a trick on her?

She waited.

The silence was terrible. She could hear her heart pumping. A bead of sweat slid down her bulbous forehead. Very slowly she bit into her crisps.

Creak.

Suddenly a terrifying thought entered Annie's mind: *Something was coming up the stairs.* And every time she took a bite it took another step, as if trying to disguise itself under the noise of the crisps!

Annie wanted to cry out, but what would happen then? The thing might run all the way up and burst through the door and get her and suck her brains out through her nostrils and ... and ... but wait, maybe it was just her parents ... But surely they wouldn't do something like this, would they?

For the first time in her life Annie Brig didn't want to play computer games, she desperately wanted to be somewhere else, anywhere but in her room. She listened again.

Creak.

It was definitely on the stairs.

Creak.

She swallowed her crisps.

Creak.

Her heart pounded.

Creak.

A bead of sweat dripped off her nose onto her trembling fingers.

Creeeeeeeeeeeeeeeeeeeeeeeeeeeak.

Whoever it was, or whatever it was, had reached the top step.

How could she defend herself? It *must* be a practical joke. Her father would say something any minute.

And then something horrifying happened. The handle of her bedroom door slowly started to turn. Something wanted in.

Annie was shaking. Sweat was pouring down her red cheeks. Her mouth wobbled.

The door stayed shut. It was locked! Locked! She remembered locking it! Thank goodness! She was safe. But whoever it was, was still there ... just metres away.

Creak.

It was moving again.

Creak.

Was it going?

Creak.

It was.

Creak.

Back down the stairs.

Creak, creak, creak. All the way down.

Had it gone?

Her ears strained to hear between her wheezy breaths. The window and door were locked. The curtain was drawn. She listened for what seemed ages without hearing anything apart from a passing car. The clock struck eight-thirty. She logged off and let out a sigh of relief.

Phew! It was gone. She was exhausted.

Who had it been? A burglar? Someone from school playing a practical joke? But how had they got in? Thankful that the threat had passed and curious to know where it had come from, Annie heaved herself out of her chair and waddled over to the door.

She inserted the key and turned it. Click. The door was now unlocked.

She slowly turned the handle, took a breath and pulled the door quickly open.

Nothing.

Phew!

Creak.

An explosion of fear surged through her. It was still there! *And now there was nothing between her and it!*

'AAAAAAAARGmmmmmmm ...' Annie's scream was cut short as a monstrous black tail twisted itself around her body. Within seconds the tail had pulled her across the landing and down the stairs into a gaping black hole.

Annie Brig had gone.

Chapter 20

On the Wings of Eagles

'Action!' shouted the French dice and the shark surged towards Kevin.

Suddenly, a pair of talons reached down and clamped themselves around his small frame. The talons plucked him into the air, safe from the snapping jaws of the shark.

Kevin gave a cry of alarm and looked up. A huge eagle was carrying him into the sky. Its powerful wings lifted him higher and higher. Kevin clung tightly to the talon, relieved to have been rescued from the shark, but terrified at being carried by the huge bird.

The eagle circled and dropped like a missile. Cold air rushed over Kevin's cheeks, his legs trailed helplessly behind him. With a piercing scream, the eagle sailed over the glassy lake. Kevin could see the King standing on the far shore, shaking his fist at him; he could see the dice bobbing up and down, shouting angrily; and he saw the bear smiling. Then they were gone and the lake was left behind as the eagle soared into the sky. Kevin tensed, waiting for the bird to drop him. But it didn't. It held him firm and secure. The eagle had come to save him.

Higher and higher flew the eagle and strangely enough, the higher they flew, the more Kevin began to relax. Each beat of the eagle's wings was calm and peaceful, the air warm and silent. Kevin watched the lake and mountains disappear as they entered a bank

118

of clouds. The clouds looked soft and firm, but when he reached
out to touch one, it filtered through his fingers. Then they were
above the clouds. Up and up they climbed. As Kevin looked back

he could see the clouds beneath him, but as they flew further away he realised they weren't clouds at all they were the pages of a book. Higher and higher flew the eagle. The book grew smaller and now Kevin could see that someone was holding it. It was Martin! And there was Randolph and the Library and all the other books.

Now he was flying higher still. The books and Library faded from view until there was just space and stars. The stars twinkled like a celestial choir and soon a multi-coloured dust shimmered through them. Never had Kevin seen anything so beautiful. The eagle broke through, creating swirling patterns of colour. It swept Kevin downwards to a small stretch of golden sand that nestled, like a streak of beckoning sunshine, on a shimmering sea: a secluded tropical island in a galaxy of stars at the end of all worlds.

A minute later, Kevin stood on the island. The eagle hadn't said anything. It had just put him down and flown away. Kevin leant against one of the palm trees and took a deep breath. He couldn't believe what had happened. He'd been rescued by an eagle and carried into space! Cheesy and Spotty would never believe him.

The island was surrounded by water, which stretched out about as far as a swimming pool before mysteriously dropping away. Kevin was puzzled. Where did the water flow? If he waded out and swam over the edge, would he be able to swim under the island and back up to the other side? Or would he fall into space?

He abandoned his thoughts and slid down the trunk of the tree onto the sand with a soft thump. The white grains slipped between his fingers but one small grain stuck to his palm - one tiny speck separated from all the others, isolated and insignificant. He knew how that felt. Looking up into the vastness of space, he suddenly felt very alone.

'But you're not alone,' whispered a voice.

Kevin jumped up and waved his hands in front of him like a panicked Kung Fu fighter.

'Please,' said the voice, 'don't be frightened.'

Kevin stared at an indentation in the sand. Something had been sitting next to him ... an *invisible* something! He shuddered and clenched his fists.

'Who's there?' he gulped. 'Who are you?'

'Don't be frightened,' the voice was calm and peaceful. 'I'm your friend. I brought you here. I'm the Panaginip Bayan.'

Chapter 21

Back in the Library

'Shhhhh!' soothed the Panaginip Bayan. 'Listen!'

'What for?' replied Kevin suspiciously.

'Don't speak, just listen!'

Sand crunched beneath Kevin's feet as he shifted his weight. Water lapped against the shore, a palm branch creaked.

'Listen harder!' encouraged the Panaginip Bayan.

There was another sound: a faint drumming noise, many drums, as if an unseen army were moving across the sky, beating on the stars with their boots as they marched. The marching grew louder and louder, until it surrounded him and now it was in him, lifting him, carrying him. He floated forwards, arms outstretched. The floating felt as natural as if he'd always been doing it and he found he could twist and turn quite comfortably.

'Open your eyes.'

Kevin thought his eyes were open already, but somehow he could open them again. He realised he wasn't on the island anymore - he was floating hundreds of feet in the air, surrounded by yellow books.

'I'm back in the Top Secret section of the Library,' he exclaimed, beginning to understand. 'I must never have left it. I must have been stuck in that book and now I'm not.' He looked at the Library floor far below. 'That's funny,' he thought, 'I'm not the least bit scared either. I suppose I should be, but I'm not ... Hold on! What's that?' A small black object was zooming up from the floor at high speed. It made a sudden change of direction and flew toward him. A familiar figure stood on top.

'Randolph!' Kevin cried, recognizing the gibbon straight away. He gave a wave, but Randolph didn't wave back.

'He hasn't seen me!' panicked Kevin. 'He's coming straight for me. He's going to hit me ... Look out!' But the craft didn't hit Kevin, it flew straight through him and out the other side, as if he was a ghost.

'He can't see you,' the Panaginip Bayan explained. 'He doesn't know you're there.'

'Am I dead?' asked Kevin, worried.

'No, you're very much alive,' laughed the Panaginip Bayan, 'but I've made you invisible, like me, so I could bring you here to show you something. Watch!'

Randolph brought his craft to a halt, leant over and pushed a book onto a shelf. The machine gave one of its gentle hums, reversed and disappeared down another aisle.

'Get the book Randolph just put back,' instructed the Panaginip Bayan.

Kevin floated over and scanned the books. 'It must have been this one,' he said excitedly, pulling a book from the shelf. 'It's got my name on!'

'Open it,' said the Panaginip Bayan. 'What do you see?'

The first page was blank, so Kevin turned to the second. A tiny light twinkled in the middle of the page.

'I'm not sure,' said Kevin, 'It's a light ... I think it's a star ... it's growing. No, it's a planet ... green and blue ... it's Earth!' He could see ice caps and continents with Europe at the top. There was England, and in the middle was a large, grey building with a leaning turret. In the turret, peering up through a skylight was a boy with orange hair. It was him - or he thought it was. The boy was ten feet tall and looked very confident.

'Yes, it's you,' said the Panaginip Bayan. 'The real you before the Dream Stealer stole from you.'

Kevin was shocked. 'Stole from me? Stole what?'

'Your confidence,' the Panaginip Bayan explained. 'He did it a long time ago. Confidence is something the Dream Stealer's good at stealing. He wants you to believe that you're useless so that you just give up. But you're not. Remember where Randolph found your book? In the Library basement? It was I who told Randolph to put it there for safe keeping until you got here. You see, your book's rather special because you were made for adventure.'

Kevin's eyes widened.

'I have chosen you specially. You're the one - the chosen one - and your adventures are only just beginning!' laughed the Panaginip Bayan. 'Don't believe the Dream Stealer's lies. He wants to keep that book you're holding empty. But I've chosen you to fill it with adventure. You're special. *Remember* that.'

> **'You're special. *Remember* that.'**

'Adventure?' A thrill of excitement surged through Kevin. He wasn't good at Maths or English, but he loved adventure.

'Turn the page,' instructed the Panaginip Bayan.

Kevin could see a small, frightened face, half hidden by shadow, moving across the open pages of the book. 'It's Misty!' he exclaimed.

'And she's in danger! ... So your next adventure, Kevin, is to rescue her. And one other thing: the moment you see her, you must both escape the way she came ... *don't forget*. Now touch the page.'

Kevin watched, amazed, as walls of steel zoomed towards him.

WHOOSH! WHOOSH! WHOOSH! KTHUNK!

As if generated by a computer programme, a metallic world started to create itself around him. Within seconds he was no longer in the Library, but in a huge industrial factory.

Chapter 22

Trapped

Occasional jets of flame and sparks spat from jutting pipes of all shapes and sizes. Hissing steam erupted at random intervals from a network of grids that ran in square sections beneath his feet. Kevin could taste the metallic vapour in the air. Above him gantries and walkways criss-crossed like neatly arranged spider webs. And then, between two immense industrial cogs, a door slid sideways and a small figure emerged, blinking and rubbing her eyes.

'Misty!' Kevin rushed over. 'Are you alright?'

She smiled and gave him a big hug, making him glow with pleasure. 'You'll never guess what's happened to me!' Misty quickly explained how she'd been trapped, how she'd met Plob, and how he'd helped her escape by dropping a stepladder into her pit before running back into the caves.

'That's where we have to go!' urged Kevin, suddenly remembering what the Panaginip Bayan had told him, 'Back the way you came.'

'Into the caves?' Misty looked horrified. 'But that's where I've escaped from.'

'We have to!'

'No,' Misty shook her head. 'You don't understand. I can't! Andy, tell him!'

'Eh? Did someone say me name?' A small green blob of jelly

popped out from Misty's top pocket wearing what appeared to be a little cap and an upside down moustache. 'It's me! Andy, Andy with an 'e'! And I forgive tha for not recognizing me,' continued the green jelly in a squeaky voice, "cause I'm in *disguise*!' The jelly removed its moustache and gave Kevin a big wink.

'Meet Andy the slime-bug,' chuckled Misty. 'He helped me find my way out of the caves.' Looking at the bug she added, 'Andy, you'd make all my friends at school laugh. You're so much fun! I wish I could take you to school with me and sneak you into lessons.'

'School!' chirped Andy. 'I'd love school ... if I knew what it was ... Is there school in Yorkshire? By gum, I love Yorkshire. They're right friendly in Yorkshire, not that I've been there ... but if I did go, I'm sure they would be. They 'ave toad-in-t'-hole in Yorkshire, don't they? Aye, I know that. Don't ask me 'ow. Well, tha can if tha want, but I wouldn't know ... I like toad-in-t'-hole, or I think I do. It's a bit like lettuce, int it? Right nice and green like me. Now where were we? School! ... What is it, anyway, if it hit me in t' face?'

Kevin laughed and told Misty about the Panaginip Bayan. 'He sent me here to rescue you,' he explained, 'He said we had to go before it was too late!'

'Rescue me from what?' asked Misty, puzzled.

A hollow laugh interrupted them. It wasn't a nice laugh, but a deep throaty 'I-know-something-you-don't-know' evil laugh, the type that mad scientists practice for hours in front of their bathroom mirrors. A figure stepped from behind a large cog; a figure the children had last seen in the Library; one that was pointing a large claw.

'It's 'im! It's 'im!' shrieked Andy in fright, hastily pushing on his moustache and disappearing deep into Misty's pocket.

'It's him! It's him!' mocked the shrunken figure, bowing low to the floor. There was a horrible clicking noise beneath Azmo's robe before he rocked back his hooded head and laughed hysterically. 'What's wrong? Expecting someone else? The Panaginip Bayan perhaps?'

Kevin felt a terrible sinking feeling in his stomach. He'd been too slow - and now they were trapped.

Azmo saw the miserable look on Kevin's face. 'So, what lies has the Panaginip Bayan been telling you? That you're special? Well, don't let it get to your head - he says that to everyone!'

A quiet cough from Misty made Kevin look up. She was nodding at the open door - there was still a chance to escape!

Azmo twisted his arm at a strange angle, snapping a final ligament into place. 'I, on the other hand, am totally trustworthy. I'm the Dream Stealer - as regular as clockwork, deadly as cancer!'

They edged towards the door.

'Bow and I may spare you ... but I think not!' Azmo spun away from them, causing his robe to flare out dramatically. 'I don't care for children. In fact, they disgust me!'

They were nearly there.

'Leaving so soon? Oh, I hope not!' The wizard's claw appeared from beneath his robe and fizzed with energy.

SHUNKKKK! The door slammed shut.

'Not before the fun begins!' Azmo tutted. Again his claw sparked. This time the children were whirled high into the air. They kicked helplessly as Azmo floated across the grid floor beneath them.

'Now let's not panic!' chirped Andy. 'We're only suspended twenty feet up o'er metal grid that'll slice us into million pieces if we fall - and that's if he doesn't decide to squash us or turn us into something 'orribly nasty like verucca, not that I've seen verucca, not 'aving any feet that is ... Oh! *See how high we are*! See how high we are! Oh, by gum! That is high, int it! Pheweeeeeeeeeeeee!' It had suddenly dawned on Andy just how high twenty feet actually was and so, turning an even lighter shade of green, the bug gulped and disappeared back into Misty's pocket.

Kevin watched the Dream Stealer gliding back and forth beneath them. Was this really the end? If so, it was his fault. He'd let everyone down. A beep interrupted his despairing thoughts. Kevin gazed at his watch, wondering why it was making noises now.

< REMEMBER >

A text message? But only Misty knew his number. Who could it be from and what was it he had to remember? Suddenly, everything the Panaginip Bayan and Randolph had told him came flooding back and a wave of confidence surged through him.

'Rubbish!' Kevin shouted, making Misty jump. '*You're* the liar! We *are* special! We're special ... and we can do something you hate we can *dream*!'

'Oh, really!' shrilled Azmo, shooting up from the floor as if propelled by an invisible rocket. 'Really?' he shrieked, bringing his hooded face inches from Kevin's nose. 'Think you're clever, don't you? Yes, that's why I hate you - because we know what dreams do, don't we?' A long globule of yellow spit flew from the hood onto a nearby pipe. 'Dreams change the future! The past is the past, but the future ... the future is uncertain ... changeable. The future is mine to control and I don't want anyone to change it with their pathetic dreams, least of all children. Why, if two of you start to dream, then more of you might, and before long the whole universe would be one happy family. Yuck!'

Misty watched the spit drip slowly onto the metal grid far below.

'Leave us alone!' she said, trying to be brave.

'Oh, tut tut!' whispered Azmo, bypassing Kevin and hovering in front of Misty. 'You still don't understand, do you? I steal dreams!' A round yellow orb, dripping with pus and smelling like rotten cabbage, glided from Azmo's hood. It was his eye. It surveyed Misty with glee, soaking up her terror like a sponge. 'And the easiest people to steal from are children. But not all children are little goody-goodies with dreams and good intentions. Some unwittingly work for me.' The eyeball did a sort of loop the loop, before retracting in disgust, disappearing into the hood with a loud slurping noise, followed by a squelching pop, like the noise a

frog makes when it gets sucked up a Hoover.

'What do you mean, "children work for you?"' asked Misty. 'How could anyone do that?'

'Quite easily, my dear! You see whenever a child is jealous or greedy, whenever they lie or are mean or do anything selfish, they're working for me! In fact, some of them get so good at it that I recruit them. I develop them. I feed them. I nurture them in my pits until they mutate into fully-grown monsters - and then I use them. I use them to make others feel miserable. I use them to steal more dreams. I call them my "pets". And I would like to introduce you to one of them ... one of my favourites. I call her "the Annihilator"!'

Azmo zoomed to a nearby walkway and pushed a large red button. With a dazzling display of flashes and bangs the floor split apart and from the caves below emerged a blue-veined mountain of blubber. The monster arose with all the grace of a lump of jelly. Blubbery folds of skin slurped over the edges of the rising platform as it was propelled upwards by straining pistons that squealed like a herd of constipated elephants. Its single eye opened wide as it saw the children. It rumbled with pleasure.

Chapter 23
You are What You arc on the Inside

The monster swayed from side to side.

Misty shuddered, 'What is it?'

Azmo's voice cut through the noise. 'Her name is Annie Brig. She was once a child like you, but a very selfish one. She was so good at being greedy and selfish that I recruited her. I went and ... how shall I say ... "fetched" her. Then I grew her in one of my pits and now, at last, she has ... *exomorphasised*! Know what that means? Of course not!' Azmo shook his head in pretend horror at their blank faces. Children were so ignorant these days ... just the way he liked it! It made them easier to deceive. 'Annie Brig has exomorphasised ... turned herself inside out ... or, if you prefer, she has become what she was on the inside!' Azmo's voice changed to a soothing patter. 'And I believe she hasn't been fed for at least five minutes. She looks very hungry and ... oh ... she seems ... to ... be ... looking ... at ... you! Oh dear!'

> **'She has become what she was on the inside!'**

'It's not over yet!' said Kevin bravely. He could see objects wedged in the monster's oozing skin: a chocolate wrapper, empty crisp packets, a mix of wires and a joystick. What had started as a hobby for Annie had become an obsession, consuming her until it had *become* her. And in the middle of all the wires and fat was a gaping hole: a wide, foul-smelling pit of greed that wouldn't be satisfied.

'Thtop! Thtop right now!' shouted a voice, making everyone look up. Plob was standing on the walkway above, holding a large, green, knobbly book. Azmo froze as he saw the book. Plob muttered a short sentence and waved his arm.

BANG!

There was a flash of blinding light, a puff of yellow smoke, and Misty and Kevin span through the air, straight into Annie Brig's flabby flesh.

SCHHUULLKKKK!

The skin rippled. With all the power of a snapping elastic band, the children shot from the blubber like an exploding zit. Kevin flew upwards, away from the disappointed chops of Annie Brig and down onto a startled Azmo.

OOOOOF! He plunged his outstretched leg straight into Azmo's midriff. Azmo's black cloak quivered violently before pitching backwards, flipping over the guardrails, right into the Annihilator's waiting mouth.

GULP! RUMBLE! BELCH! A greedy smile spread across what could only be called the remnants of Annie Brig's face.

'Ee by gum, the Dream Stealer's gone! Just like that!' Andy's eyes peaked from Misty's top pocket. 'That were easy, weren't it! Slime ball! ... No, I didn't mean that, 'cause I like slime, I love slime, I *am* slime ... but I didn't like '*im*!'

'Andy, thank goodness you're alright! I was worried you'd got squashed.' Misty scrambled out from the pile of boxes on which she'd landed.

'I was, Misty. I was indeed. Squashed flatter than pancake I was, no ... even flatter! It was as if blue whale 'ad used me as cushion. But tha know us slime-bugs, we don't break, we just bend and splurge, and after a bit we return to our natural shape. Sorry about pocket though. It might take three washes to get stain out. I *were* frightened after all!'

Kevin happily tickled Andy's chin. 'I'm glad you weren't in *my* pocket!'

But Misty didn't hear Kevin's last remark, because she'd spotted a familiar figure - their rescuer!

Plob smiled. Master had underestimated him. He'd even surprised himself. He was still shaking with nervous excitement at what he'd dared to do: secretly tip-toeing into his master's cave, stealing the magic book and creating a dangerous explosion spell to rescue the Misty creature and her friends.

Misty wrapped a thankful arm around Plob and gave him a big kiss on his forehead. Big tears welled up in Plob's eyes. It had been worth it. He was no longer a mouse, he was a special somebody - a hero.

'Ahem!' coughed Kevin. 'Isn't there something we've forgotten?'

'Like what? Fully automatic camcorder to capture this happy moment?' piped Andy excitedly. 'Not that I've ever seen one, or even know what one is ... No, what 'ave we forgotten? ... Cuddly toy? ... To blow our nose? ... To pack our suitcase? No, I don't know, I'm as flummoxed as nun in beauty parlour ... what 'ave we forgotten?'

'That!' said Kevin pointing over Misty's shoulder.

All three turned slowly. A sickening, sinking feeling settled in their stomachs. Following the line of Kevin's quivering finger, they came face to face with the drooling jaws of the Annihilator. There was no escape.

Like a monstrous wave, Annie's lips arced overhead, engulfing the entire walkway, trapping them in walls of slobbery blubber. Kevin flinched as Annie's wet tongue wrapped around him, pinning his arms to his side. Her hanging eye twitched, a globule of saliva dripped from the roof of her mouth and her body shook excitedly. The others watched helplessly as Kevin was lifted into the depths of Annie's mouth.

BANG!

A second explosion rocked the cave. Sticky goo peppered the children's faces as they cart wheeled across the room. Annie Brig had exploded.

They clattered to the floor. Something Annie had eaten hadn't quite agreed with her - and that something was a small, wizened figure of rage and evil. Azmo had survived his journey into Annie's

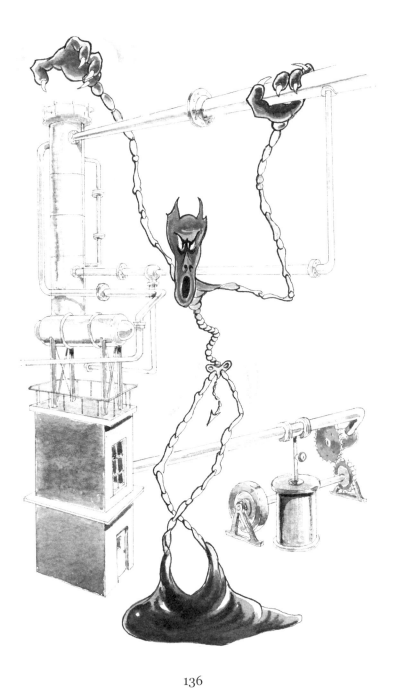

136

digestive system. Worse still, he was furious.

All around the factory, layers of lard dripped in gloopy globules. Misty and Andy lay dazed. Annie's hydraulic lift juddered and vibrated on its damaged pistons. Plob was nowhere to be seen. Old, dusty papers from the spell book fell from the air in a steady stream. Some were on fire and as they burned, bolts of energy were released like zapping laser beams, melting holes in walls, turning pipes into spitting snakes and making whole floor panels disappear. Other magic pages fluttered to the ground only to be transformed into an assortment of vegetables, animals and weird wizard things: a bouquet of flowers, a pink rabbit, a medieval shield and a chair of pure gold. It was unnerving. But worst of all, through all the chaos, Kevin could clearly see the hunched figure of Azmo: a twisted, spindly, skeletal, yellow figure who no longer wore his robe. A figure Kevin would have felt sorry for if he hadn't known the evil that lurked behind those piercing eyes; eyes that now scrutinised him with intense hatred.

Kevin began edging back towards Misty and Andy. They had to find a way out whilst they had the chance.

'RAAAAAAAAAAAAAAAAAAAAAARRRRRGGGGGHHH!'

Kevin froze.

Azmo's neck was stretching. Up and up it went, higher and higher. A loud snapping noise accompanied each new vertebra as it extended itself, swaying high into the charred air. And now the arms were stretching, shooting sideways like unravelling bony coils of rope. Next it was the legs. Up they went as if an invisible child were placing building blocks one on top of another at an incredible speed.

'RAAAAAAAAAAAAAAAAAAAAARRRRRGGGGGHHH!'

Again Azmo screamed.

His wiry frame lurched to and fro like a ridiculously tall and spindly rubber man. The bendy arms and legs swung wildly around the tiny body like swinging acrobats. And, far above, the piercing angry eyes remained glued to Kevin.

Azmo, with a swing of his arm, reached into his mouth and yanked his tongue.

WHOOOOOOOOSHHHHHHH! With all the speed of a ripcord-inflated life jacket, Azmo expanded into his full demonic glory - a cold, reptile-looking, multi-fanged, three-hundred-ton monster.

Misty screamed. The monster raised its scaly head skywards and roared. The noise was deafening. The factory floor shook violently. A flame burst from its nostrils, igniting the roof, bringing a couple of metal pipes crashing down around them.

And then, with a speed that surprised them all, it turned and lowered its blackened head. Knowing eyes bore deep into Kevin. This was no ordinary monster. It was the Dream Stealer, exomorphasised.

Chapter 24

How Azmo had a Blast

Azmo's scaly head drew back as he inhaled a deep draught of air, getting ready to roast his victims alive with a blast of fiery dragon breath.

It was at that point that everything seemed to go into slow motion for Kevin and as if someone had switched off the sound. Through all the fluttering pages and dripping flab he could see Misty's mouth opening and shutting as she screamed in terror. Plob's knees were knocking and Andy was doing his best not to faint as Azmo's nostrils flared in preparation for the killing blast. On the floor just in front of them something caught Kevin's eye. It was the medieval shield that had come from the wizard book. He knew it was their only chance. Instinctively, he forced the corner up with his foot and heaved the large shield forwards to protect them just in time.

WOOOOOF! A ball of scorching fire hit the shield, causing it to tremble and glow red-hot. The heat seared through Kevin's hands, making him cry out with pain. The blast was so intense that the nearby pile of boxes burst into flames, causing a cloud of smoke to billow out in front of them.

'Quick! Misty shouted, peering round the shield into the thickening smoke. 'Run!'

Plob stood frozen to the spot. His mouth was quivering. 'M ... m ...

mathter ...' he stammered pointing at a claw that had appeared in the smoke.

'Come on!' whispered Misty, yanking Plob out of his stupor. 'He's not your master any more! You're *free*!'

Andy bounced up and down in her pocket as they ran. 'Faster! Run faster! Ee by gum, I think we've got as much chance as last cherry tart at vicar's tea party! Ooo, this running is bumpy, int it? It's worse than sitting on pneumatic drill ...' Andy paused as he saw Plob's bemused look. 'If tha don't know what pneumatic drill is, which I don't, it's a big drill that's filled with air like kind of wind I just did ... Oh! ... Tha didn't want to know that did tha ... well I *am* scared. We all are, aren't we? ... My goodness gracious, that smells! Oh! Look out!'

'Duck!' screamed Kevin, pulling Plob and Misty to the floor. He watched Azmo's tail, like an immense black tentacle, whip in a wide arc and crash against a pile of machinery. A cloud of dust and grit showered down, making him cough, and a couple of aluminium pipes crashed to the floor, narrowly missing their toes. A monstrous shape flew overhead making everyone duck again. Misty looked at him helplessly. Kevin seized one of the pipes. It had a jagged point at one end that made it look like a spear. 'Come on, arm yourselves!'

'Eh? What do tha mean?' replied Andy. 'I can't lift one o' them! All I've got is this stupid moustache. What can I do? Tickle him under t' chin? Now if I 'ad crossbow ... 'ang on ... what am I saying? Sure I can pick things up, but stretch crossbow, knock an arrow and pull trigger with no hands? Come on! Who do tha think I am? Incredible Hulk? I know I'm green ... but not *that* green! Stretching bow would split me in 'alf ... 'ang on ... *two* Andys? That's not bad idea, is it? ... "'ello Andy, 'ow are tha?" "All right! 'ow about thee?" "Smashing! Kettle's on. Cup of tea?" "Aye!" "Two sugars?" "No! Cutting down!" ...' Andy stopped and stretched a fold of slime to point skywards at a swooping shadow. 'Watch out! 'Ere he comes again!'

Azmo's sleek, scaled body soared through the smoke like a black bullet with razor teeth.

WOOOOOF! A second blast of fire caught them unawares, scorching the shield black and sending them all sprawling. In the sudden confusion a huge claw reached into the smoke. It plucked Misty into the air, lifting her, screaming, high into the factory roof, with Andy stuck underneath the claw, beating valiantly at it with his false moustache.

Kevin and Plob watched aghast through a gap in the smoke. The dragon soared in a wide circle before landing on a metal gantry, five hundred yards above, with a loud CLANG, squashing Andy flat. Andy didn't mind too much - after all, he could always reform himself later - it was just that having a three-hundred-ton dragon standing on him wasn't the most comfortable feeling in the world.

'Eeee! I'm stuck in right jam!' chirped Andy from beneath the monstrous claw. 'Not t' jam in jar ... though I do look bit like

marmalade just now! Sorry, Misty, I can't help tha nowwwwww.'
Andy's chatter was cut off as Azmo made a deliberate point of
leaning on that claw to squash Andy even flatter.

Misty was no better off; she lay between the dragon's front claws.
Azmo yawned and lay his head on the metal walkway. At the far
end was a metal staircase that zigzagged all the way down to
ground level. A flicker of a smile crossed his scaly face and he
looked at Kevin invitingly. The girl was the perfect bait. He closed
his eyes; he had only to wait.

Misty knew it too. She could see Kevin looking up at her through
the smoke. 'Don't!' she whispered. 'Don't come up here! It's a trap.
He wants you to. Don't do it!'

She let out a helpless moan as first Kevin and then Plob started up
the steps. She could see Kevin carrying the pipe and Plob the
shield, but what use were they against a three-hundred-ton
monster? She glanced at Azmo's face. His breathing had slowed
and his eyes were closed, but she had a fearful feeling that
somehow he was still watching. Very slowly she reached for her
phone, trying hard to ensure the dragon didn't notice. She began
to text a warning to Kevin. Why was he being so dumb? Couldn't
he see it was a trap?

Kevin breathed hard as he climbed step after step. He was terrified
and wanted to run away, but he kept going. Misty needed his help
and as long as there was a chance, he had to try.

And, anyway, the dragon looked fast asleep.

Chapter 25

Showdown

Kevin stepped, panting, onto the end of the gantry and as he did, his watch beeped.

< IT'S A TRAP >read the text.

Azmo's eyes flicked open, but as Plob stepped up behind Kevin they narrowed in hatred. Azmo glared at the dwarf who had betrayed him. Blasting Plob would be too good an end for him - he deserved something else. A wry smile crossed the dragon's face as he pointed his claw.

BANG!

A cloud of red smoke enveloped Kevin, making him cough. He aimed his makeshift spear against the approaching dragon but Azmo hadn't moved; he was laughing at the small animal standing next to Kevin. The creature gave a swish of its tail, a clumsy turn and a distressed whinny. Plob had been turned into a donkey!

Azmo snorted with glee. Why had he never thought of turning Plob into a donkey before? It was so obvious! Azmo licked his lips. And now he would eat the stupid creature.

Plob plopped himself onto his bottom. He looked pitiful. A donkey! He'd been turned into a donkey. He wasn't 'Plob the mouse' anymore, but 'Plob the donkey!' His ears drooped down in front of his round hazel eyes. He'd been laughed at and picked on for years - he'd got used to that. The problem was he'd begun to

hope he could escape. But now he was worse off than before. He should never have started hoping; it was too painful. Tears welled up in his eyes. Hoping and dreaming were a waste of time. He tossed his grey shaggy head, shaking off Kevin's comforting hand, making his mane wobble. Kevin didn't understand. No one did.

'Now then!' squeaked a faint voice from beneath Azmo's claw. 'Just look at thee now - right swanky in posh grey suit with full set of gnashers and swishing tail. I've always fancied a tail. Imagine that! Andy slime bug wi' tail! I'd make me friends right jealous. I'd 'ave tail and they wouldn't. I could swish it and wave it and if I got bored I could ... I could swish it again. Aye! I wish I 'ad tail!'

Plob paused. He hadn't thought of it like that.

'That's right!' cried Misty, seeing Plob's droopy ears. 'Don't give up! There's still a chance. We can still escape!'

Plob opened his eyes. Misty was still hopeful. Perhaps he could be too. He pricked up his ears, gave a loud snort, jumped to his feet and banged his hooves down hard on the walkway. Yes, he would hope a little bit longer! He looked up at the big dragon that had made his life a misery for so long and then back to his tail, which swished defiantly. Quite a nice tail really! He dipped his back to Kevin, inviting him to climb on. He would do what a donkey could do. The moment Kevin was sitting comfortably with the shield in one hand and the spear in the other, he turned to the dragon and made a loud donkey noise.

Azmo nearly fell off the walkway laughing. It was ridiculous. The boy and the donkey were going to attack him. All he had to do was flap his wings once and they would charge beneath him and over the edge to the factory floor far below. It was a showdown he would enjoy.

He rippled his scales in anticipation.

Kevin raised his shield.

Plob swished his tail.

Azmo's eyes narrowed with hatred.

Plob snorted.

Kevin gripped his spear.

'Come, noble steed,' he muttered. 'We have a dragon to slay!' With a squeeze of his thighs he urged Plob forward. Plob needed no urging. After three hundred and seventy-five years of misery this was a battle he was ready for. His hooves thundered along the metal walkway; his mane streamed behind him

Kevin grasped the shield tightly, lowered his spear and took aim; but there was something in the way that Azmo was shifting his wings that made him feel uneasy.

Azmo crouched lower. The fool had committed himself. Another few yards and it would all be over. He would leap up and the boy would plunge to his doom.

Misty watched helplessly.

Azmo tensed. Any second now ...

At the very last second Kevin twisted backwards. Letting go of the shield, he readjusted his grip on the pole and with all the skill of an Olympic javelin thrower, hurled the makeshift spear.

Azmo sneered, he had overestimated his foe ... the boy was stupider than he thought! He sniggered. All he had to do now was rise into the air, catch the spear in his claw, reverse the point and use it to humiliate the boy by impaling him on his own weapon.

But ...

Azmo had *under*estimated how sticky a squashed slime bug could be. His eyes widened in surprise as he tried to leap but found that his foot was temporarily glued to the spot ... just long enough for the javelin to hit its target ...

SHHHHHHHHUUUUK!

146

With a squeal of pain Azmo wrenched his foot free and spiralled upwards. His talons reached up to tear the lance from where it was embedded in the base of his shoulder. Flapping uselessly on one wing, he tipped sideways. He scrabbled helplessly at the gantry. For a moment he managed to hang on by a single claw. His yellow eyes glared in hatred before opening wide in alarm as his claw gave way. With a terrified scream the dragon plunged to his death.

Plob braked hard, digging his hoofs into the walkway and sending Kevin catapulting into Misty, who was knocked, screaming, over the edge. Kevin snatched at her hand, just managing to get a hold of her wrist. He gasped with pain as she swung beneath him as he lay stretched like an elastic band, clinging to the rail with one arm, holding Misty with the other. He looked into her petrified eyes, round with fear, pleading with him to hold on, but he knew he couldn't. His arm was shaking. His knuckles had gone white and his fingers were slipping ...

And then something caught his eye. A claw had suddenly appeared on the edge of the walkway, ten yards away. *Azmo was still alive.*

As Azmo had fallen, part of his wing had trapped in the metal scaffolding. He had managed to twist around, wrench free and slowly climb back to the top, where he was determined to devour the children and his faithless servant, Plob. With such thoughts filling his mind Azmo hauled himself over the edge of the walkway, only to be met by the backside of a grinning donkey.

THWACK! With an almighty kick of his back legs, Plob's hoofs rammed into Azmo's snout, whipping the dragon's head back with a loud crack.

STOMP! Plob's hoofs slammed down onto Azmo's claws. Instinctively, the huge dragon let go. He scrabbled desperately … but it was to no avail. With a cry of alarm and rage he fell, head over heels. Andy peered over the edge, watching the dragon tumbling through the smoke. For a moment he thought he saw Azmo's body turn to its original weak, spindly form, before dissolving into a green vapour and disappearing into the factory smoke.

Seeing that Azmo was finally gone, he turned to help Kevin and Misty.

'Nearly there!' cried Andy, sliding over to them. ''Elp is on its … oh 'eck! Where've they gone?' Plob let out a whinny of despair.

They were too late. Kevin and Misty had fallen.

Chapter 26
How Dreams Shape the World

Kevin kicked and waved wildly. His insides were screaming. The factory was spinning. He could see the floor far beneath him ... then Misty ... then the ceiling ... then the floor - a floor that rushed to meet him faster than he could think.

But instead of crashing *into* the concrete floor, Kevin and Misty dropped right *through* it!

With a shimmer and a loud splash, they plunged from the factory world into a sea of salty water.

Down and down they sank. But instead of getting darker, the water got lighter and lighter. The next thing they knew, their heads had broken the surface and they were gulping mouthfuls of fresh air as they bobbed up and down in the warm water.

'We're alive!' Misty panted, excitedly. 'Kevin, we're alive! We're not dead! What happened? I don't understand!' She gazed disbelievingly at her new surroundings.

Kevin pushed back his dripping hair and helped Misty wade out of the water. He was back on the island, the strange island suspended in the middle of space with its two palm trees and golden sand. But there was something else this time ... something that hadn't been on the island before.

A cat was staring up at the stars and it was only when they were both standing next to him, that it turned its head towards them.

'Welcome to my island, Misty Gilmore,' said the cat softly. Misty was surprised to hear her name.

'Don't you remember me?' purred the cat to Kevin, 'In the Forbidden Turret? It was I who jumped through the skylight to help you find the key. I brought you here - both of you.'

'That was you?' Kevin was puzzled. 'But what are you doing here? I don't understand.'

The cat began to grow. It grew bigger and bigger until it had turned into a fully-grown black panther - a very large black panther that was twice as large as any big-cat Kevin had seen before. There was no point in running away because there was nowhere to run, and, anyway, there was something magical about the panther, something beautiful about its green eyes which seemed to see right through him and know everything there was to know.

'Well done,' said the panther, gazing at Kevin, 'Well done for being brave and rescuing Misty, but most of all, for not giving up. Your adventure has been tough, but that is the making of you. When others would have given up, you didn't.' Kevin didn't know what to say. He felt pleased and a bit awkward. Misty put her arm around him, proudly.

The panther was changing. It was shrinking, getting smaller and smaller until it was the size of a beetle. Misty blinked in disbelief.

'I'm the beetle that helped you in the Library!'

'What do you mean?' Misty was confused. 'We didn't see any beetles in the Library!'

'Yes,' said Kevin, crouching down to speak to the small creature.

Its tiny antennae wiggled back and forth like a pair of miniature hands waving up at him. 'We saw monkeys and gorillas ... but definitely no beetles!'

'Who said anything about seeing?' buzzed the beetle. 'It was I who chewed through the leg of the bookcase ... Have you forgotten already? ... The bookcase that fell on Azmo! It was I who made it fall!'

Kevin was puzzled. What did the beetle mean? Without warning, the beetle started to grow and within seconds it had changed to a majestic eagle.

The huge bird towered over the children. It turned its head sideways, gazed down at Kevin and spoke with a voice as awesome as its appearance. 'It was I who rescued you from the dice!' The eagle lowered his eye to within inches of Kevin's face and whispered, 'I am the Panaginip Bayan.' The bird stepped back, stretched to its full height and spread wide its impressive wings. 'Remember? It was I who sent you the text. I brought you here for a reason.' And then, pausing to look at Misty, it softly said, 'And I also brought you here.'

The eagle shimmered and rippled like a reflection in a pond, transforming its golden frame into a giant mirror, in which Misty could see her reflection. She gasped because she looked so beautiful. 'Misty,' said the Panaginip Bayan gently. 'I brought you here to help you understand that it doesn't matter how well you do at school, or what your parents think, you're beautiful just the way you are. From now on you're not to compare yourself to Cynthia Slogitt.'

Misty bowed her head.

The mirror rippled again. Kevin stared at his orange hair, podgy fingers and sticky-out ears.

'I've made you look like that Kevin, to teach you that it's not the way you look that makes you special, it's got nothing to do with your freckles or the colour of your hair - it's *who* you are. And don't worry about your father. Everything will be alright, trust me ... I know how the story ends.' Kevin desperately wanted to ask about his father, but again the mirror was changing. Its surface swirled, transforming itself into the panther again.

The panther's green eyes looked straight into theirs. There was a long silence. Kevin and Misty felt awkward. It was as if the panther knew everything about them - all the lies and mistakes and wrong things they'd ever done, even the ones they'd forgotten about. But although they felt ashamed, they weren't scared. Opening its

> 'It doesn't matter how well you do at school, or what your parents think, you're beautiful just the way you are. From now on you're not to compare yourself ...'

153

mouth, the panther took a deep breath and roared straight at them. The roar was very loud and very fierce, but it didn't feel as if he was roaring at *them*, but at all those wrong things they'd done. The roar went on and on and on. They closed their eyes as one by one all their worries and fears and tears were blown from them. The longer the roar went on the lighter and happier they became. At last the roar stopped.

'There! They are gone,' Kevin heard the panther say. 'Gone forever! I have blown them into the depths of space. They are forgotten. They have been erased from your book. Today is a new day. I have made everything new.'

Kevin slowly opened his eyes and smiled. He wanted to jump and shout. He felt clean and happy. Misty was laughing which made him start laughing too. And the more they laughed the happier they became. The panther began leaping around them and now they were chasing him, trying to catch his tail, running around the island, ducking between the palm trees, splashing in the water and skipping along the sand.

'More!' shouted Kevin. 'More!'

'More!' agreed the panther. 'More!'

Now they were jumping and running in a circle and the more they ran the more they laughed.

'More!' shouted Misty. 'More!'

'More!' agreed the panther. 'Much more!'

Into the water they jumped, splashing each other, screaming and laughing. Eventually, after what seemed ages, they collapsed in a pile on the sand. They lay there, exhausted, either side of the panther, catching their breath.

Kevin lay on his back and closed his eyes. He'd never felt like this before. Things with his father would be alright; everything would workout for the best. The water lapped around the shore, Misty giggled and the panther purred loudly. Kevin was warm and happy. The storm, the dice and the Dream Stealer seemed far away. He remembered the Library with all the books. He could see one of the books now, as if it was really in front of him. It had a picture of Earth on the front cover and now it was opening and getting bigger and the pages were turning while the panther, somewhere behind him, was speaking.

'Your world is a beautiful place, but it needs you in it. It needs you to make your dreams come true so it can become a better place.'

The pages turned and a pop-up picture of a house jumped from the book.

'My house!' Misty said. Kevin could see her, running excitedly across the pages. Two dogs were in the garden, barking for her to come and play. She waved at him before the page turned and a second pop-up picture of an old building with a leaning turret appeared. He touched the picture with his hand and suddenly he wasn't dreaming but standing in the attic room back at Greystones.

He looked at his hands, turned them over and wiggled his fingers. They were normal! He touched his nose, felt his ears and smiled. It was nice to be the Kevin he was used to.

The room was silent, the door was open and there in the corner sat the box with its lid tightly shut - as if nothing had ever happened.

How Everyone has a Story

Of course, you're probably wondering what happened to Plob and Andy. No sooner had Kevin and Misty disappeared, then the factory shook like a giant jelly and they were transported by the Panaginip Bayan to the next stage of their journey.

Plob found himself back home in Gweeshmoor-on-the-Flat, a place that he'd longed to return to for three hundred and seventy-five long years. He was home and in the years to come there'd be nothing he'd enjoy more than sitting on the porch of his new house, sucking on liquorish sherbet twists and telling the young dwarfs of the time that he was turned into a donkey and slew a dragon.

Andy was sent by the Panaginip Bayan on another secret mission so I can't tell you where, other than to say it involved lots of slime and a wig.

Lawrence Pudding-Pig was given a three-week detention by Mr East and forced to write an essay on 'Why Stealing Strawberry Trifle is a Very, Very Bad Thing to Do'. One could say he received his just desserts!

Kevin told his friends, Spotty and Cheesy, all about his adventures, and Spotty was so excited that he talked non-stop about them for three whole days. Together they began to write down their dreams and plan what they want to do in the future.

One of Kevin's dreams is to discover who the strange lady is whose picture is on the back of his watch - that's an adventure for another time. Kevin also e-mailed Misty and was delighted to read that she'd got her first A+ in English for writing an essay on dragons.

Meanwhile, back in the Library, Randolph eased himself into his chair, picked up a hardback yellow book and placed it gently on his knee. He opened the cover and looked at the blank page. Perhaps one day the child whose book it was would start to dream. And the moment they did, words would appear and their future would start to be written.

He wondered why so many children didn't dream. Perhaps they didn't know how special they were or realise the power of their dreams.

He was glad Kevin and Misty had found out. He shut his eyes and smiled. It was nearly time for supper and tonight he'd make sure all the monkeys received extra helpings of Chocolate Mousse Surprise.

A note from M.D. Griffiths

Isn't it amazing that there's a book with your name on, sitting on a shelf in the Future section of the Library, waiting for you to start dreaming? A dream, remember, is something that you would like to happen one day. It's something specific that you can write down and, when it happens, you can tick it off.

What are your dreams?

Is it to play for a great sports team? Is it to have your own horse? Do you want to go surfing? Perhaps you want to become a zookeeper, or be a good mum or to meet someone?

Your dreams are powerful because they pull you into your future, into what you were born to be.

The following is from a book, found in the Library of Knowledge. Here are ten ways to stop the Dream Stealer stealing your dreams!

⟶

Wisdom

- from the
Library of Knowledge

1. Dream

It doesn't matter how big or small your dream is, as long as you have one. People with no dreams don't know where they are going and just drift aimlessly through life. This world needs you to dream your dreams because, by dreaming and accomplishing them, it will become a better place.

You can have hundreds of dreams, but let's start with five. Write down five dreams that you have now and don't read on until you've written them down.

1..

2..

3..

4..

5..

2. Do what you're good at doing

(which is probably what you enjoy doing.)

There's no point in dreaming to be a tennis player if you can't hit a ball. There's no point in auditioning to be a pop star if you can't sing. But you are good at something and even if you don't know what it is right now, it's just waiting for you to discover it. Maybe you're good at swimming or art or smiling and being friendly.

What are you good at doing?

3. Do something about it.

If you want to be a footballer you need to go out and practice. If you want to be a computer genius you need to start learning to use your computer (but not just playing games like Annie Brig!) Start taking small steps to achieve your dream. No one achieves dreams overnight. Dreams happen one step at a time.

What one small thing can you do today?

....

....

....

4. Don't compare yourself to other people.

Misty was wrong to compare herself to Cynthia Slogitt. You can't be someone else and they can't be you. Are you trying to 'fit in' and be like someone else? If so, stop it! Just be you! Andy is Andy, Kevin is Kevin, Misty is Misty and you are you.

Next time you look in a mirror, look yourself in the eye and confidently say 'I am special'. And then keep saying it every day.

5. Who you are on the outside is determined by who you are on the inside.

Andy, though small on the outside, had a big heart that was full of joy. If you were exomorphasised who would you really be? Lots of people appear to be rich and confident and trendy on the outside, but aren't on the inside. What's inside really does count and will one day show. Have a good heart, tell the truth and be the best person you can be! It always, always pays!

6. Hang out with good people

Apart from your family, who are the three people you spend most time with? (Write them down before you carry on reading).

1..

2..

3..

If I told you that you'll end up like them, would you still want to hang out with them? If you hang out with losers like Lawrence Pudding-Pig you'll become a loser. Hang out with great people like Andy and you'll be great. It's that simple!

7. Stay away from 'dream stealers'.

'Dream stealers' are often cunningly disguised. They look nice on the outside, yet all they want is to steal your dreams.

Has anyone ever told you, 'You can't do it' or that 'You're no good' or 'You're ugly'? Listening to negative words steals dreams.

Messing with drugs and cigarettes steals dreams - they steal your health and money.

TV is a big dream stealer - it steals your time.

Don't listen to those negative words. Don't mess with drugs.

Don't waste your wonderful life in front of the TV.

Watch out! Don't let the Dream Stealer steal your dreams!

8. Never, never, never give up.

Don't be disappointed if things don't go as you plan. They never do. Don't blame your parents, don't blame the government, don't blame yourself. When things go wrong (and they will) keep going! Don't allow the slimy Pit of Despair to get you down. Most people's dreams don't come true because they give up too easily. Do you want your dreams to come true? Then never, never, never give up!

9. Remember that your book is in the Library.

It's sitting on the shelf, waiting to be written, waiting for you to start dreaming.

It sits with billions of other books, all part of one big library. We're all in this wonderful world together, so make sure some of your dreams help others, because they're the best dreams of all!

What are you going to do for someone today?

10. Remember how special you are.

Kevin went through a whole load of stuff that just wasn't fair. The storm and the dice and the shark weren't fair. But life isn't fair. So when stuff happens to you and you don't feel special, just smile and remember you are - you really are!

No one else is going to achieve your dreams for you.

Write them down, believe you're special, be confident and go out and achieve them and make this world a better place.

But always beware ... of the Dream Stealer!

To order further copies visit:
www.mega-u.com